# NAKED MANHATTAN

## Carl U Maxwell

Naked Manhattan
By Carl U Waxwell
Copyright © 1985, 2026
Cover art by Gemini/Adobe
ISBN print: 978-91-90010-57-0
ISBN e-book: 978-91-90010-55-6
Published by Yabot AB, Sweden, 2026

# CHAPTER ONE

I never wanted to be a fucking cop.

All I ever wanted was to be a mechanic—grease under my nails, torque wrenches singing, the sweet smell of oil and exhaust instead of this piss-soaked precinct stink.

My old man was a cop. His old man was a cop. And his old man probably rode with goddamn Wyatt Earp. The badge is in the blood, they say. I say it's a curse.

So here I am, Jack "Hard" Harlan, thirty-eight years old, NYPD Midtown South, 23rd Precinct. We got a real paradise going in this city. Three police commissioners in four years, more racial conflicts than a Klan cross burning on Times Square, no money to keep the fucking Plymouths running, and the most burned-out, underpaid collection of civil servants east of the Hudson.

Most days I feel like I'm busting my balls for zero. I collar some punk on a nickel bag, and by the time I finish the DD5 he's already back slinging on the corner. That kind of justice gives a man an attitude.

My attitude got me shipped down to Missing Persons. Punishment detail. Siberia with fluorescent lights.

I keep wondering if I'll ever crawl out of this hole. Unless I turn up Jimmy Hoffa's concrete shoes in the next week, the odds ain't good. Mechanic dreams are for suckers who still believe in happy endings. So I guess I'll just keep eating this shit sandwich.

The phone on my desk started screaming. Because I'm a prick who can't leave well enough alone, I picked it up.

I was praying it was Captain Malloy telling me I was canned.

I was praying it was some fed saying I made next Wednesday's Most Wanted. I knew better. It was just another asshole who expected me to do my goddamn job.

Why couldn't it be Tina begging to crawl under the desk and suck me off while I pretended to work? My cock twitched just thinking about her hot mouth. What a waste of a hard-on.

I sighed and barked into the receiver.

"Harlan. What do you want?" I said.

The voice came back thin and nervous. "I need to file a missing persons report."

"Yeah?"

"Yeah."

I was already thinking, So file it, dipshit, and leave me the fuck alone. I hate this job and I don't give a rat's ass about your problems.

No such luck.

"Okay. Who's missing?" I asked.

"My brother."

"How long?"

"About a week."

Goddamn it. The rule book says twenty-four hours and we gotta look. I wanted the days to stretch out forever, but I wasn't getting that wish.

I tried anyway. "Look, pal, most people who disappear

want to disappear. They don't want to be found. You got any reason to think your brother's hurt?"

The voice whined louder. "Hank—that's my brother—and I have lunch every Thursday. He didn't show. The lazy fuck won't cook for himself and he's too cheap to buy his own burgers. You bet your ass something happened."

This guy and his brother were already pissing me off.

I went for the kill. "Maybe Hank finally found some pussy and he's balls-deep somewhere. Maybe he got sick of you buying him lunch at the McDonald's on Flatbush. Maybe he got lost on the BQE and he'll turn up in an hour. Hell, maybe Hank got a sex change and now he's your sister."

Silence. Then: "You don't know my brother, so quit talking like a fucking asshole. It's your job to find him. Find him."

Looked like I was doing my job.

"Gimme your name and address. I'll send someone out to take the report."

"Fred Rossi. 4567 18th Avenue, Bensonhurst."

I scribbled it down, hung up, and started the impossible hunt for any breathing cop in the squad room to take this call.

Hernandez was on a buy-bust. Chapman was at the fucking dentist. Morales and Ramirez were out shaking down Times Square girls, and Captain Malloy was in his usual throne: the shitter.

The Captain's tropical fish were staring at me from the tank. The janitor was mopping. No badges in sight.

Where the fuck are the cops when you actually need one?

The janitor reminded me he wasn't sworn, so this steaming pile was mine.

I sat there kicking my heels together under the desk. I didn't want this case. Missing people want to stay missing. They're sick of the old lady's nagging, the kids screaming, the bill collectors calling at dinner, the same green shag carpet staring back at them every night. They want out. They want to disappear. And the last thing they need is some underpaid city drone sniffing around their new life.

I cleaned off the desk, swallowed cold coffee that tasted like battery acid, shoved a stale sandwich down my throat, and stood up. The job was mine whether I liked it or not.

Didn't Fred Rossi know I didn't give a flying fuck about poor Hank?

Didn't he know I had better things to do—like not being here?

I thought about my old man and knew why I stayed. Being a cop beat being dead. Barely.

Okay. Fine. I'd swing by Tina's walk-up in Hell's Kitchen first, get my pipes cleaned, then head out to Brooklyn and listen to Freddy whine about his lost brother.

I was a horny bastard. If I don't get laid regular I turn mean. Skip lunch with Tina and everyone in my path gets a busted nose.

My pants were already tenting at the thought of her. I glared at Malloy's fucking fish and knew it was time to blow this dump.

Tina is the hottest piece I've ever had—and brother, I've had plenty.

I've never been above letting a Times Square hooker slide to her knees in exchange for a quick blowjob behind the Port Authority.

You don't like it? Tough shit.

The courts spit them back out in an hour anyway. Might as well get the best head on the planet second only to Tina. Why lock up prime talent when you can bust a nut twice a day for free and the bitch thanks you for the privilege?

Maybe you're dumber than I thought.

But no woman—black, white, fat, skinny, ugly, gorgeous—has ever come close to Tina. She can drain me five times before breakfast. Her tongue's so hot a corpse would rise up and beg for one more round. He'd shoot so hard he'd blast himself right out of Hell and into paradise.

If I could quit sleeping I'd be balls-deep in her twenty-four seven. In the squad room. In the back of the cruiser. Anywhere she'd hold still long enough.

I hauled my sorry ass down the precinct stairs, fighting the urge to stroke myself through my slacks. Poor Fred Rossi was ancient history. All I could think about was the last time Tina and I fucked.

Christ, what a woman.

The picture burned in my skull. Me flat on her futon, cock so hard it hurt. Her velvet tongue dragging down my stomach, circling the head like fire. Blood roared in my ears. I'd blow the second she didn't stop.

I didn't want her to stop.

That tongue slid from the swollen tip all the way to the root. Her teeth grazed the shaft—sharp little sparks shooting straight up my spine.

I was losing it. Wanted to paint her face white.

She kept licking. Flicking the slit. Her hands cupped my balls, rolling them while her mouth pumped the length.

No holding back. Hot jets of come flooded her throat. She swallowed every drop like it was champagne.

I shook the memory loose and hit the parking lot like a bull in heat. Had to cool off before I exploded.

My department Plymouth sat there like a tired old whore—five years old, two hundred thousand miles, no tune-up in eighteen months because the city spent the budget on more jail beds instead of keeping wheels turning.

Great plan. You can't lock anybody up if the cars won't move.

I slid behind the wheel. The bastard wouldn't start. Typical. God bless New York City.

Fuck this car. Fuck this job. I wanted pussy and I wasn't about to play mechanic on this heap to get to Tina's. I'd taken the train in that morning anyway, so I headed back to the subway. I'd file the repair ticket later.

The trains are a circus—late, filthy, stinking of piss and desperation. You sit there calculating how long it'll take to walk the rest of the way. Drug deals in the open. Hookers working the cars. Flashers. Robberies. The shit you see could fill a soap opera.

I was gonna get that repair request filed fast.

I wanted off that train worse than anything.

Except I wanted my tongue buried in Tina's cunt even more.

The twenty-minute ride took two fucking hours.

Some scumbag decided the old lady in the back had Social Security money in her purse and tried to snatch it. If he'd just offered to fuck her she probably would've pulled out her rosary and thanked Jesus. Instead he grabs her check and I spend two hours giving statements to the uniforms before they cuff the dirtbag and cut me loose.

Being a cop means you're never off duty. See a crime, report it. All I wanted was a fast lunchtime fuck and I got stuck in a goddamn episode of Dragnet.

I wondered what fresh hell was coming next. Maybe I'd trip on the sidewalk and get flattened by some gang kid on a hot skateboard. Maybe I'd drop dead of a coronary. Maybe some goddess would step out of the steam vents and beg for my tongue.

Maybe I'd get to Tina's alive and find her in bed with her girlfriend.

No. I couldn't be that lucky.

Could I?

# CHAPTER TWO

I could.

Tina lived in one of those cheap-ass new walk-ups they slapped together all over Hell's Kitchen. Green lumber, shitty appliances that broke if you looked at them wrong, three-bucks-a-yard carpet that smelled like cat piss the day they laid it, and some bullshit French name on the awning to jack the rent to five-fifty a month. They throw up two hundred of these firetraps in six months, and seven years later the city uses the charred skeletons for training drills.

Tina's place was still fairly new. It hadn't collapsed yet—give it time. For five-fifty you'd figure the walls would be thick enough to muffle the boom-boxes blasting salsa, kids screaming, couples slapping each other around, and the wet slap-slap of some chick getting her cookies next door. No such luck. I heard it all the second I pushed through the street door.

I'd been after Tina for over a year to ditch this plastic shithole and move in with me on Avenue C where the roaches pay rent and the heat works maybe twice a winter. Real people, real life. She wouldn't budge. This broad was dynamite in the sack, but when it came to real estate her brains were somewhere up her tight little ass.

I got to her door and found it cracked open. Moans and wet sucking sounds spilled out into the hallway.

That was my Tina. If there was pussy or cock on the menu, she was already ordering seconds. Born dripping and ready. Some days I wonder how the hell I keep up with her for even ten minutes. She'll rip through ten orgasms in an hour, then twenty fucking minutes later she's grinding her snatch on my face again begging for round eleven. Every guy should have a piece like this.

Tina swings both ways hard. Loves a sweet juicy cunt on her tongue almost as much as she loves wrapping those hot pink lips around a throbbing dick.

I don't give a shit if she eats pussy. Hell, I love watching it. Gets me rock-hard every time. When I was fourteen I walked in on two bitches going at it in the girls' john at school—been hooked ever since.

I followed the sex noises straight to her bedroom. Her little side piece Val was face-deep in Tina's snatch and Tina was loving every filthy second of it.

I stepped through the doorway just in time to watch Tina slide her dripping honey bush up Val's chest. Her swollen pussy lips shone with juice, slick trails gleaming across Val's heavy tits.

I hung back and watched.

Tina kept grinding her cunt against Val's blazing tongue. I could see Val flicking the tip right on Tina's clit. Tina moaned like a bitch in heat, hips rolling, "Eat me. Oh fuck, I love your tongue. Lick me. You're so goddamn good. Kiss my pussy. Kiss my fucking pussy. Make me come. Make me come. My cunt's on fire. I'm burning up. I want you. I want your tongue."

Val's face was soaked in Tina's sweet honey. I could almost taste it from where I stood.

Val reached up and grabbed Tina's tits, pinching those ruby-red nipples between her fingers till they stood out stiff. Tina's whole body jerked in raw lust. She arched hard and gasped, "Suck my tits. Roll my nipples between your lips. I want your hot tongue on my tits. Feel how hard I am. Nobody does it like you. Suck me. Suck me."

I knew she was seconds from blowing. I'd seen Tina hot plenty of times, but Val had her wound so tight I thought she might fucking explode.

Tina couldn't keep quiet. She kept bucking her hips, love juice shining on her puffy lips.

She glanced up, saw me, and gave me that look—look how good I'm getting it. "She's gonna make me come. Her tongue's so fucking hot. Jack, I want to come. I want Val's tongue on my clit. I want to feel her."

Val answered with a wicked grin, "No. Not yet. I want you to suffer. I want you hot and horny and begging. I want to watch your passion climb while I tease you with my mouth. I want your pussy hotter and hotter." Tina's eyes flashed panic—she was right on the edge.

Val pulled her mouth away from Tina's clit and licked her lips slow. She wasn't done torturing her yet.

Val slithered up Tina's belly, dragging her tongue through the wet bush, over the stomach, up to those swollen tits. She rolled to the side, flicked her tongue across one hard nipple. Back and forth, the bud swelled darker, harder. Then she sucked the whole tit into her mouth, rolling the nipple between her teeth. Tina's back bowed off the futon.

Val wasn't stopping there. She shoved three fingers straight into Tina's steaming box. Tina bucked instantly, "Fuck me. Fuck me with your fingers. Make me come with your hand. Harder. Push harder. Shove your whole fucking hand in me. I want to feel you fuck my pussy." I watched Tina's cunt muscles clutch at Val's hand. She was hotter than I'd ever seen her, frustration boiling over as she begged, "No more. Let me come. Stop teasing. I'm gonna die. Oh God."

What she really needed was my cock.

I stepped to the side of the futon, unbuckled, dropped my pants. My twelve-inch prick sprang out rigid, pointing straight at Tina's gaping pussy like a heat-seeking missile.

Shirt hit the floor. I slid onto the bed.

I grabbed Tina's ass, shoved a finger up her tight asshole, started fucking her there while Val kept finger-banging her cunt. Tina pushed back on both holes, couldn't decide which felt better. Her soaked pussy pulled away from Val's hand, then slammed back. She rolled side to side in a frenzy. "Oh God. I can't take this anymore. Somebody make me come before I die."

I yanked Val's fingers out of Tina's dripping hole and licked the sweet juice off them. Too much. I had to taste it straight from the source.

I pulled my finger from Tina's ass, buried my face in her cunt. Her passion poured down my throat. She was on fire.

Her clit throbbed under my tongue. I flicked left-right-left, relentless. She arched up, grinding into my mouth. Blood pounded through her cunt as she begged, "Eat me, Jack. You bastard. You love my pussy, don't you? You want to rub your tongue on my clit? You like my hot juices in your mouth? Taste me. You can't live without fucking me with your mouth. Tell me you like it. Tell me you want me to come on your face."

I kept stroking her with my tongue. Her passion kept climbing. I was gonna make her come so hard the neighbors on the next block would hear it. Tina shoved up against me and exploded. Spasms gripped my tongue as I plunged my fingers back inside her. Love juice gushed out. "I'm coming. Oh God. You feel so good. Suck me harder. Suck me harder and fuck me with your hands. Oh God. Fuck. Fuck. Oh Jesus."

Tina collapsed, spent. I slid my hands out of her box and crawled up her body. My throbbing cock begged to push between her lips. Her mouth opened wide.

Her tongue wrapped around my rod. She was already hungry again.

I pushed up on my knees, straddled her face, started rocking, fucking her mouth deep. Each thrust sent my cock sliding down her throat, her tongue dragging along the shaft. I was so hard I thought I'd snap.

The jism boiled up fast. I was gonna blow. Hot pulses shot into her mouth. I started to pull out; a few thick ropes splattered her cheeks. Her tongue darted up, catching every drop.

I rolled off, collapsed beside her. But Val wasn't done. "My turn now, Jack," she said.

After watching us, Val was so hot she'd have fucked a gear shift on the BQE.

She reached over, cupped my balls, fingernails pinching the sensitive skin. I started hardening again.

This time I wanted them both.

Val slid her hands under my ass, pushed a finger into my hole. I wanted her mouth on my cock.

I looked up at her. "Suck me, baby. Wrap your hot tongue around my cock."

Val dove right in.

Her tongue slithered down my chest till it hit the head. She flicked the ridge, light as a feather, but the heat was pure fire.

I was gonna die from the tension.

"Put it in your mouth, honey. Swallow me whole." Her hot mouth closed over me.

This broad gave the best head I'd ever had. I kept pushing deeper, hitting the back of her throat, still not deep enough.

I was close again. I clamped the base hard. "Stop, baby. Not yet. I want to fuck you. I'm not ready."

I stroked myself a couple times, but then Tina's hands were on my balls, rolling them gently. She looked at Val. "Get on his cock. Put your hot pussy on his dick and let me watch you fuck him. I want to see you make him come in your cunt."

Val was ready. She leaned over, shoved one fat tit in

my mouth, and slid down onto my cock. Her pussy was an inferno.

She started slamming her hips down. I sucked her swollen nipple, bit it hard. It stiffened even more. Heat poured out of her box.

Her cunt gripped me like a fist. She started coming fast. "You asshole. You fucking prick. Fuck me with your cock. Harder. Harder. Ram it all the way through me. Make me come. Fuck me till I come." Spasms milked my shaft. "Oh God. Fuck me harder. Harder, you bastard. I'm coming. I'm coming."

Val collapsed on my chest. Now Tina wanted it.

I rolled her under me, lined up, shoved my throbbing meat into her dripping hole. I pounded in and out; she rose to meet every thrust.

"Fuck me. I want you to fuck me. Your cock feels so good. Fill me. Fill me up. I want you deep inside. I want you to come in my pussy. Fuck me. Fuck me."

I went faster, harder. Grabbed her hips, slammed in blind lust. Nothing else existed—just her flaming cunt wrapped around me.

I couldn't hold it. Her pussy begged for it. I buried it to the balls.

Tina slid her burning cunt up to meet me. My load splashed against her walls. "You're so hot, baby. I want you. Your cunt's on fire. You're the best. I love fucking you. You make me come so hard. I love your fuck hole."

Tina's juice ran down my softening shaft. I rolled off, lay there gasping.

My prick lay dead between my thighs while Tina and Val rubbed my back, trying to drag me back to earth.

Sweat soaked me. Muscles limp.

I wondered what the hell I'd done to deserve this kind of action.

I turned over, pulled one on each side—Tina left, Val right.

I kissed them both.

I knew they'd set this up just for me.

Tina knew I couldn't make it through the day without pussy. Knew I'd swing by to bury my face in her snatch sometime before the shift ended.

Bitch.

She had my number.

Val was the bonus for the tongue-lashing I'd given Tina that morning. She'd come at least ten times already and was still dripping when I had to drag my ass back to Midtown South.

The fucking precinct.

My cock twitched again. I leaned over, shoved my tongue between Val's lips. I was ready for another round.

No fucking way.

I knew the brass would have my balls if I didn't get back. I was a civil servant. Job to do.

Fuck the precinct.

Fuck me if I didn't drag myself back.

Fuck Missing Persons. Fuck Freddy Rossi and his missing brother.

I wanted more pussy.

Who gave a rat's ass about Hank? Not me.

Later.

The phone company was threatening to cut me off. God bless Ma Bell.

Who wants to answer the phone with his face buried in a horny snatch?

I kissed the girls again, watched them wrap around each other. Told them I had to go look for some faggot who didn't want to come home for dinner, and I'd be back later ready to tongue their swollen cunts again.

I climbed off Tina's futon, got dressed. Tied my shoes staring at Val's tits. Life's a bitch.

I started out the door, heading for the subway, when I heard Tina whisper to Val, "Tramp."

She had my number. I hoped she'd keep dialing it.

# CHAPTER THREE

It hit me like a brick when I realized I had to drag my sorry ass back to the precinct on the fucking subway. Me, a civil servant, riding the goddamn trains like some broke-ass schmuck. The city couldn't keep a decent mechanic on payroll to save its life.

They should've hired me. We'd all be better off.

Here it was the middle of July, heat rising off the asphalt like a furnace, and I'm trudging to the subway entrance like a welfare case. If the city spent half as much on keeping cars running and less on chasing Times Square hookers who'd be back on the stroll in an hour anyway, none of this shit would happen.

Wishful thinking from a guy still leaking pussy juice down his thigh.

I sat on the platform bench wondering what Fred Rossi would have to say. The train was late—big surprise—and I started thinking Freddy might have to point me to another piece of tail. When the graffiti-covered car finally screeched in, I crammed myself next to some homeboy who wanted to brag about his next score. I tuned him out. All I wanted was to see Fred, wrap up his bullshit, and get back to my girl's sweet wet cunt. The last thing I needed was another collar.

The train spat me out two blocks from the Midtown South Precinct lot.

I walked over to the battered Plymouth the city tries to pass off as my cruiser and turned the key. It coughed, laughed, then died.

Fuck it.

I pushed through the squad-room door and caught Captain Malloy glaring at my empty desk like it owed him money.

Captain Malloy is the most disgusting slab of meat I've ever seen walking upright. He squeaked past the five-foot-six height requirement by half an inch and tipped the scales at two-forty easy. That greasy red beard hadn't seen scissors since cops rode horses. He smelled like a dumpster behind a Fulton Fish Market stall on a hundred-degree day. Worse, he ran the squad like a dead rat—slow, stinking, and useless.

It didn't take a genius to figure out why he was camped at my desk.

"Hey, Captain. What the fuck you doing at my spot?"

"HARLAN," he belched, "where the hell you been? You got a fucking job."

I thought about telling him the truth—been balls-deep in a hot piece of ass—but the fat fuck didn't have the brains to understand lust. Hell, he probably couldn't piss without soaking his own shoes. "Had an errand, Captain."

"My motherfucking ass. You're here to protect the citizens of this city. Don't forget it."

"That's exactly what I was doing." Protecting two horny broads from terminal frustration.

The Captain slammed his sausage fingers on my desk. "Some asshole's been blowing up the phone for three hours looking for you. You were supposed to see a guy named Fred Rossi about his missing brother. You never showed. That ain't police work, Harlan."

"Yes, sir. I was headed out there, but the fucking cruiser's dead in the lot. What was I supposed to do—hitchhike?"

"You could've grabbed another car if you weren't so busy chasing tail from that little chippy of yours."

"There wasn't one."

"Bullshit. Take mine and go see this citizen. Solve his problem. You're a representative of this department. Don't forget it."

How could I? At least the prisoners got out someday.

I snatched his keys and headed for the lot. The only decent ride in the fleet—the Captain's personal sled. No trouble getting to Bensonhurst.

Fred Rossi lived in one of those tired old row houses squeezed together like they were afraid to stand alone. The kind of block where the stoops were cracked, the paint peeled, and the tiny front patches they called "gardens" were mostly weeds and cigarette butts. Urban renewal hadn't hit here yet—probably never would.

Freddy met me at the door with a scowl that could curdle milk. "Where the fuck you been? If somebody was breaking in, I could've been dead by now."

I barely heard him. Behind him stood this gorgeous blonde, about five-ten, stacked to the rafters, pouty red lips, legs that went on forever, and a look that said she needed cock yesterday. This broad was something else.

I tried the cop routine, but all I wanted was to throw her down and do the let's-fuck routine. "I'm Harlan, NYPD Midtown South. Somebody named Rossi called about a missing brother."

The blonde answered, "You mean my Uncle Hank. Daddy called."

Daddy growled, "Yeah. Four fucking hours ago."

Fred pulled the door wider. I stepped in and watched the world's finest ass cheeks sway away from me as she drifted toward the back of the house. I wanted to grab those globes, knead them hard, then bury my tongue deep between them. No such luck—

Fred turned to her. "Bianca. Go occupy yourself while I talk to the officer."

She gave me a slow, filthy smile over her shoulder before disappearing up the narrow stairs.

I crossed the room, dropped into a recliner, pulled out my notebook. "Now, Mr. Rossi. You wanna report your brother missing?"

The interview dragged on the same way—Freddy bitching about his brother vanishing, the side piece, the fat wife who wouldn't put out, the untouched bank accounts, the car in the garage. Same story, same frustration.

But every few minutes Bianca would reappear in the hallway just beyond Fred's line of sight. First she leaned against the doorframe, arching her back so her tits strained the thin blouse. Then she turned sideways, letting me see the hard nipples poking through. Next time she hiked her skirt an inch higher, flashing smooth thigh and the barest hint of lace. Each time she caught my eye she bit her lip, ran a finger along her collarbone, or cupped one breast like she was offering it.

My cock was throbbing against my zipper the whole damn time. Fred kept yapping, oblivious.

Finally I wrapped it. "Got a picture of your brother?"

Freddy glanced toward the stairs. "Hey, Bianca! Grab a picture of your Uncle Hank for the officer!"

She called down she'd get it.

I stood. Fred stood. He stuck out his dead-fish hand. "Thanks. I'll keep my ears open, but do your fucking job."

I gave the handshake, already turning for the door.

Fred scratched his gut. "Shit, I gotta run down to the corner for smokes. You need anything else from me?"

"Actually," I said, keeping my voice level, "I should probably talk to your daughter too. Maybe she's got something on Hank she didn't wanna say in front of you."

Fred snorted. "Doubt it. Kid barely knew him. But if you wanna waste your time, she's probably up in her room. Top of the stairs, door on the right. Just don't let her talk your ear off."

He shuffled out the front, muttering about the price of Kools.

I took the stairs two at a time.

The door was cracked. I pushed it open.

Bianca was waiting.

She'd changed. Black lace bra that barely held her heavy tits, matching thong that disappeared between those perfect cheeks, sheer black stockings clipped to a garter belt, no shoes—just those long legs and a hungry stare. She stood by the bed, one hip cocked, fingers already tracing the edge of her thong.

"Thought you'd never get up here, Officer," she purred. "Been teasing you all through Daddy's bullshit. Did you like the show?"

I kicked the door shut. "You're playing with fire, sweetheart."

"Good. I want to burn."

She turned, bent at the waist, and slid her hands down her thighs, spreading her legs so the thong pulled tight against her swollen lips. Blonde curls peeked out the sides. Moisture already darkened the lace.

I stepped up behind her. She reached back, grabbed my wrist, guided my hand between her legs. My fingers found soaked fabric and hot flesh. She ground against my palm.

"Watch me first," she whispered. "I love being watched."

She straightened, turned, sat on the edge of the bed, spread her thighs wide. Red nails hooked the thong aside. Perfect pink cunt opened for me—swollen clit, glistening slit, begging.

"Watch me make myself come. My pussy's so hot. I want to rub my clit and make it explode. I want to feel my cunt squeeze my fingers. I want to play with my pussy for you. Tell me you wanna watch me come."

My cock ached. "Show me, baby. Rub that pretty cunt. Let me see how horny you are."

Two fingers plunged in. Another circled her clit. Hips bucked. She fucked herself faster, ass bouncing on the mattress. Juice coated her hand, dripped down her crack.

I dropped to my knees for the close-up. Her heat hit me like a wave.

She shoved a finger up her tight asshole, sank down on it, rubbed her clit harder. "I'm gonna come. You wanna see my pussy come, don't you? Wanna watch my cunt pulse just for you? My cunt's on fire. Feel the heat?"

"Yeah, baby. Come for me. Show me that pussy. Come hard."

She shattered. Juice gushed. Asshole clenched. Body shook like she'd been electrocuted.

When the spasms slowed she crooked a wet finger. I sucked her fingers clean—sweet, musky, pure sex.

I unzipped. Cock sprang free.

She lay back, legs wide. I pushed in slow. Virgin-tight walls gripped me like a fist.

"Oh God, baby, you're so fucking tight. Sweetest pussy I ever felt."

I thrust deep. She moaned. "All the way inside. Harder. Fuck me. Make me come on your cock."

I pounded. She bucked up to meet me. "I'm gonna come, baby. Your pussy's too hot."

"Pull out," she gasped. "Come on my pussy. On my belly. I wanna watch it shoot."

I yanked free. Thick ropes painted her blonde bush, her flat stomach, her heaving tits.

She was still quivering. I pressed a finger to her clit, rubbed.

"You're gonna make me come again. Rub my clit. Shove your hand in. Feel me come."

She convulsed a second time, screaming my name.

I collapsed beside her, stroking that soaked bush, wondering if poor Freddy had any clue what a filthy little exhibitionist his daughter really was.

She pushed me gently. "You better split before Daddy comes back."

Smart. NYPD detective caught balls-deep in a citizen's daughter? Career-ender.

But she looked up, eyes still hungry. "Come back and fuck me again?"

I pinched her swollen lips, shoved my tongue down her throat. She knew the answer.

I slipped out, down the stairs, past the empty living room. Fred was still gone.

I was already looking forward to the encore.

# CHAPTER FOUR

My shift was done.

Fuck. My whole damn life was done. Being a cop is brutal work. Pounding pussy three times in one day is brutal work.

Bianca, Tina, and Val were just gonna have to let one of New York's finest catch a goddamn breather. Captain Malloy could have his heap back tomorrow. I was heading home.

Home was a crumbling Victorian walk-up on Avenue C in Alphabet City. Junkies nodding on the stoop three doors down, working girls turning tricks right under my window, a torched bodega across the street for scenery, and the constant scream of sirens, car horns, and fistfights to lull me to sleep.

Why do I live here? Keeps things interesting.

The Captain's Plymouth looked ridiculous in my cracked driveway—all its glass intact, current plates, no fresh bullet holes. I wasn't worried. By morning it'd blend right in with the rest of the neighborhood: ready for the crusher.

I shoved the front door open (lock busted again, same as always) and stepped into my bare-bones cave. Never been big on furniture. Couple of beat-up recliners, a sagging couch that smelled like wet dog, two lamps that flickered when the BQE trucks rolled by, a fridge that rattled like tuberculosis, and a mattress. Why fill the place up just to make more shit to clean?

I shuffled to the fridge, yanked out a Schaefer, and dropped my wrecked carcass into the recliner in front of the twelve-inch black-and-white. I knew I had to call Tina, but Christ, I couldn't even get it up to dial. I was fucked out. I knew she was gonna be pissed I didn't show, and I really didn't want to hear her mouth. But I didn't have much choice. I reached for the phone.

The bastard rang four times before she picked up, breathing heavy already. "Hi."

"Hi, baby. What's shakin'?"

I knew damn well what she was doing. Probably sprawled on that futon in her Hell's Kitchen walk-up, legs spread, fingers busy. Nice picture for my head, but my cock wasn't buying tickets tonight. She was gonna have to take care of that hungry cunt by herself.

Her answer came right on cue. "Waiting for you, Harlan. The only thing that should be up is your dick."

"I'm wiped, baby. After all that sweet pussy you fed me this afternoon, my prick's in a coma."

"Poor baby. Let me lick it back to life for you."

I would've loved to take her up on it, but I was drained dry. Bianca had sucked the last drop of juice out of me. That horny little eighteen-year-old had turned me into a tired old fuck at thirty-eight.

I tried to sound halfway human. "I'd love to, baby, but I'm just too fucking beat. I'll swing by tomorrow—save some of that tight pussy for me."

I braced for the fight, but she surprised me. "Yeah, okay. Rest up for me. See you tomorrow."

I hung up wondering who'd be balls-deep in her tonight. Her little girlfriend had probably split, and Tina never went long without finding some hard dick to ride.

Task done, I got up and slapped an X-rated tape into the VCR. Tonight's feature: *Cum-Crazed Cheerleaders* starring Bambi Blaze and Iron Dick Jamal. Fifteen minutes in, some brother had a chick strapped to a wheel, spinning her by her nipple clamps. Jesus. I killed the machine. That "hot tip" from the squad room was pure garbage. I'd leave the filthy thing on Morales's desk tomorrow with a nice note. Wondered if the little prick pulled that shit on his wife. Hoped not.

Leaning back, I couldn't shake the Rossi case. I hadn't given a rat's ass about Hank disappearing until Bianca flashed that bald little clit at me. Something in that family smelled rotten, and it went way deeper than one teenage exhibitionist.

I figured I'd have to spend some time with Hank's wife and find out what the fuck her deal was. Couldn't believe the old bag was half as bad as Fred made her out to be, or Hank would've dumped her years ago.

Unless she had something on him. That was worth chasing. No guy stays with a dried-up old bitch unless there's a damn good reason—and that reason's usually money. More important, no guy walks out on his wife with nothing but his shorts and a hard-on while he's still got a piece on the side.

There was more here than met the eye.

I wondered where Freddy fit. Looked like he and Hank were tighter than Siamese twins. He knew every dirty detail of the guy's life. Brothers aren't that close unless they're into something together. Business? Pussy? Something kinkier? Who the fuck knew. But I was gonna find out.

I didn't know how Bianca's weird shit tied in, but I'd dig that up too. No broad acts like that unless somebody taught her. Was it Fred? Uncle Hank? Interesting question. I'd start digging tomorrow. Right now I was hitting the rack.

The rack was just a mattress on the floor, but when my head hit the pillow it felt like heaven. I'd dream about cunt all night and wake up ready to tackle the Rossi brothers.

Thought about marching into Malloy's office and quitting in the morning, but nah. I had his car, a father with an attitude, and an overdue Con Ed bill. I'd ride the Rossi thing till something better came along—like my own garage.

* * *

Morning.

I didn't want to get up. Didn't want to move. My big resolution about Hank and Freddy had evaporated. I didn't want to deal with Malloy and I didn't want to play cop. I had a raging hard-on and nowhere to put it.

Considered jerking off, but since I had the Captain's

wheels I figured I'd better drag my sorry ass to the precinct.

Pissed, choked down a stale heel of rye toast, threw on yesterday's clothes, and stumbled out to the driveway.

The motherfucker was trashed. Malloy's shiny '79 Monte Carlo was fucked. Tires slashed, stereo ripped out, seats gutted, tank sucked dry. Why the hell did I think it'd be safe on Avenue C? Nothing's safe on Avenue C. Still, I was the dumb prick who left it there.

I climbed into my '49 Buick and headed to Midtown South. Skipped the usual IRT subway ride because I figured my own ride might be needed for a quick getaway when Malloy went nuclear.

The report on the Captain's wreck was gonna eat half the day anyway. Spared me from the Rossi brothers, but the shit I'd catch from Malloy made them look like choirboys. Wondered when they'd kick me back to Vice and out of this Missing Persons limbo. Hoped the transfer happened while I was dreaming about eating Tina's snatch.

I climbed the stairs to the squad room. Desk sergeant said it'd been quiet: couple runaways pinched boosting from a bodega, three dealers popped, couple burglaries. No missing persons turned up.

What else was new?

I wasn't looking forward to facing Malloy. He was gonna lose his mind over the car, and I'd be drowning in his shit for hours.

Best to rip the bandage off. I walked into his office and planted my ass in front of the desk.

He glared. "Morning, Harlan. I see you took my fucking car home. I had to ride the goddamn subway like a civilian. I said you could use it. I didn't say it was yours."

I tried contrite. "I know, sir. It got late."

He wasn't buying the choirboy act. "Where's my fucking car, Harlan?"

I could've played dumb, but the guilty-as-sin look was all over me and he was eating it up. No point dragging it out. "It got trashed in my driveway."

"My car, what?"

"Trashed. In the driveway."

"Motherfucker."

"Hey, quit talkin' to me like I did it. If this fuckin' department had decent street patrols this shit wouldn't happen."

"It's that fuckin' neighborhood you insist on living in, Harlan. I can't figure out why you stay there."

I listened to another ten minutes of motherfuckers and fucks before he finally cooled off. I thought he'd blow a gasket, but then he started making sense again. "Did you file a report?"

I lied. "Yeah. I want Auto Detail to nail the punks as bad as you do."

He bought it. "Motherfucker. What's done is done. That's why I pay those insane insurance rates. Take the cruiser and get to work. I'll deal with this bullshit later."

I figured I'd be on suspension the rest of my life, but I lucked out. Worst I'd probably get was another six months in Missing Persons. Could've been worse.

I decided to move before he changed his mind and decked me.

I dragged my feet back to my desk. Didn't want to touch the Rossi thing, but no choice. The other files on my desk were growing mold. Only thing left was to see what the hell was up with Hank.

I sat drumming my fingers, realizing I knew jack shit.

Figured I'd make use of the city's computer and see what popped on Hank. Decided to run Fred at the same time. Something about that bastard set my teeth on edge.

Ramirez ran computer ops. Guy had the personality of wet cardboard and the brain of a genius. Get past the BO, the constant farting, and the zero sense of humor, and he was a wizard. Give him a name, plate, fake SSN—anything—he'd cough up every time the guy took a dump since kindergarten. Nobody ever beat Ramirez and his machine. Once your info was in there, it never came out.

His office was down in the basement at 1 Police Plaza. I had to hoof it downstairs and across the street. Malloy passed me muttering under his breath just as I decided to go see Ramirez. By the time the Captain cleared my path, I knew I had to get down there fast.

Getting past Malloy wasn't easy. He wanted to know where the fuck I was going, what the fuck I was doing, what kind of asshole lets a car get wrecked. I didn't answer. Just kept walking. Figured I could bullshit my way through the day and avoid him again.

1 Police Plaza was supposed to be the answer to everything: extra jail space, high-tech security, room to grow. Three police commissioners in four years later, we'd had five jailbreaks and one inmate knifed. Place was overcrowded, early releases every week, no money for expansion, and the lots around it turning into parking. Civic planning at its finest.

I walked down three flights and got greeted by Ramirez's secretary.

Maria was a knockout. Five-ten, perfect size six, raven hair, hazel eyes, no freckles anywhere I could see.

I hadn't seen all of her, but the fantasy was nice. Wondered if I could talk her into a drink someday.

"Hey, Maria. What's good?"

I got one of those "that's the most unprofessional thing I've ever heard" looks. "Yes, Detective Harlan. Would you like to see Mr. Ramirez?" She wasn't in a friendly mood today. I decided to hold off on asking her out.

"Yeah. Got a couple names I need run."

She picked up the phone. As she lifted it to her ear she said, "I'll tell him you're here."

I stared at her tits while she talked. Had to be 44-DDDs pushing against that blouse. Cleavage looked ready to burst the buttons. Wondered how she breathed in something that tight. Wanted to reach over and squeeze, but she said, "Mr. Ramirez will see you now." Big fuckin' deal. Don't know why she acted like the guy was royalty. Brilliant with computers, zero everywhere else.

"I know the way," I said.

I walked past her, stole one last glance at those knockers, and kicked Ramirez's door open with my boot. "Hey, Ramirez. Got a job for you."

He wasn't thrilled. "I'm buried in shit already. This important or can it wait?"

"Guy's brother thinks it's important. Malloy thinks it's important. I don't give a fuck."

"Okay, lay it on me. I'll see what I can do."

"Missing persons case that stinks. Middle-aged guy splits, leaves everything. Brother reported it yesterday. Guy's been gone two weeks. Had a mistress and a wife who's supposed to be a real ball-buster. Haven't met her yet. Brother's a freak—his daughter's an exhibitionist. I think he knows more about his missing brother than he's letting on, but I need a place to start besides the worried wife."

"Sounds like a boring motherfucker, Harlan. Give me the names and whatever you got. Any of them have sheets?"

"Not that I know. All I know is the case stinks and I don't want to spend the rest of my life hunting this prick just so he can tell me he ain't going home."

"I hear ya. I'm slammed. Can you hold off till morning?"

"Yeah. Gotta see the wife anyway. I'll swing back tomorrow."

"Okay."

"Thanks, man."

"No problem."

I shut his door and left him with his true love: the computer. Some days I wondered if the son of a bitch had ever even touched a woman. Figured the odds were fifty-fifty he hadn't. Nobody's perfect.

Maria's tits were brushing the desk as she reached for a pencil. I grabbed it for her and got a quick look down her blouse before I left the building.

It was a hot motherfucker outside. Had to be ninety-five, humidity like a wet towel. The second I hit the street I started sweating. Grabbed my '49 from the lot and headed out to see Hank's wife.

Riding across town I wondered why she hadn't filed the report. Maybe she was thrilled Hank was gone. This interview was either gonna be gold or a total waste. With luck I'd find Hank jerking off in the bathroom at home, but the odds looked slim.

Hank lived in a decent patch out in Forest Hills, Queens. One of those new tract houses going for a hundred grand—Jacuzzi, the works. Either Hank got one hell of a deal or something was seriously fucked about him vanishing. Nobody walks away from a setup like that without a damn good reason.

I parked on the street, left it unlocked. Nobody was touching the Buick in this neighborhood.

Hank had a security gate. I hit the button and waited. Electronic buzz, then a voice: "Can I help you?"

I hate talking to machines, but no choice. "Yeah. Detective Jack Harlan, NYPD Midtown South. I'd like to talk to you about Hank Rossi."

"Yes. I'll let you in. At the tone, push the gate and come up."

I followed orders, walked to the front door. A plain woman held it open. I took the invite and stepped inside.

Place was as nice inside as out. Hank had dropped serious cash on the furniture. She pointed to a chair. I sat, feeling like a bum in church. Figured I'd do the cop routine and get the hell out.

"Mrs. Rossi, I'm the detective assigned to locate your husband."

She answered in a sharp voice. "Oh, yes. Call me Angela, please."

I went along. "Okay, Angela. First—why didn't you report your husband missing?"

"Detective, you didn't know my husband. He'd disappear for weeks. Hank and I have been married almost twenty years. He's pulled this before. I used to panic. Now I don't even worry until he's been gone a month. His brother's the one who's all worked up. There's something about those two."

"You say he's vanished before. What do you know about those times?"

"I never really knew what he did. He was a salesman when we married. I figured he was busy working, forgot to call. There was always money, so I didn't complain. By the time he got into accounting, I figured it was women.

Yes, I know he cheats. But he's a good provider and doesn't bother me much, so I let it slide."

"So you figure he was off screwing around again."

"That's what I said."

"Any idea who the women were?"

"When I was younger I cared. Now I don't want to know. Hank's life is Hank's life. Long as I'm not going without, I don't care."

Looking around, Angela Rossi wasn't going without anything. If I were a woman I might tolerate a little dick on the side for a life like this too.

"Angela?"

"Yes?"

"You said something about Hank and Fred. Something about that relationship bother you?"

"Bother me? It stinks. Hank always paid more attention to his brother than to me. Those two are joined at the hip. Always going out, hanging together. Shit, Hank spent twice as much time with Fred as with me. Excuse my language, detective. It just makes me so angry."

"You resent Fred?"

"Resent him? I hate him. You know mama's boys? Well, Hank's a brother's boy. All the years I've known him, Fred's had something on him. I can't figure what, but I know he does."

"Angela, Fred says you and Hank didn't have much of a marriage."

She flushed, got uncomfortable. I'd hit a nerve.

"Much of a marriage? Hard to have one when Hank's always with Fred. Now, if I know Fred, he told you I'm the biggest bitch alive, I hated Hank, all I want is his money. He's been saying that crap about me since I was twenty. He's got nothing nice to say about anybody but Hank and that daughter of his—Bianca."

Hot images flashed through my head. Bianca was one strange piece. Wondered what the wife knew. I asked. "I've met Bianca. Interesting girl. Where does she fit in your opinion?"

"Interesting. Nice word for it. It's okay, I know what she is. Little exhibitionist. Prancing naked around the house by five. When she hit her teens Fred had to lock her up to keep her from jumping every guy who walked in. She's why Fred's wife left."

Brilliant detective work—I hadn't even asked about the mother. And what was an eighteen-year-old still doing at home?

"You think Bianca has anything to do with Hank's disappearance?"

"No idea. I know she's trouble. That's all. I don't see why everyone's making a federal case out of this. He's gone for a while. When he runs out of cash or steam, he'll crawl back."

"So you don't think anything's happened to him."

"No. He's just out screwing around again. You're wasting your time. He'll turn up."

"You said he's an accountant. Mind if I see his files? Might be a clue."

"I don't have them here. They're at his office. Never seen them, don't know his clients. Can't imagine an accountant pissing someone off enough to vanish, but if you think it'll help, call his secretary and see if she'll let you look."

"Thanks. I'll do that."

Couldn't think of anything else. She clearly didn't give a damn Hank was gone, so why keep bothering her? I shook her hand, said I'd be in touch when I had something. She gave a warm handshake and showed me out, explaining the security would lock behind me.

I was glad to get the hell out. Freddy was right about one thing—this lady wasn't much to write home about. Since Ramirez wouldn't have anything till tomorrow and I wasn't ready to face Malloy, I decided to hit Hank's office and see if anything there pointed to where the hell he'd gone.

I fired up the Buick. Great car. City ought to buy a couple thousand of them and ditch the shitty Mopars they were stuck with. Another pervert fantasy. They'd keep running whatever junk they could get cheap.

I dropped her into gear and headed for Midtown. Worst case, his secretary was as ugly as his wife. Best case, he was cooking books for the mob and my problems were over.

# CHAPTER FIVE

Hank Rossi's office was nothing special. Stuck in a grimy Midtown tower on Fifth Avenue, it looked like every other two-bit accounting dump: beige walls, cheap metal desks, the smell of stale coffee and old paper. Old Hank had his name spelled out in cheap plastic letters on the lobby directory. Naturally he was on the fifth floor and the elevator was busted—again. Typical New York.

This case was turning into a major pain in my ass.

I trudged up the stairs. I didn't have much fucking choice.

Hank's secretary was anything but boring. The old bastard might've picked a dull wife, but when it came to secretaries he had killer taste. If I had to stare at a piece like this every day I'd never get a goddamn thing done.

If she hadn't been holding down the fort while Hank was AWOL, I'd have figured he ran off with her. As far as I was concerned, he fucked up by not doing it.

After eyeballing the broad for what felt like ten goddamn years, I walked up to her desk and slapped my shield down. "Jack Harlan, NYPD Midtown South. I'm investigating the disappearance of your boss, Hank Rossi."

"So?" she replied.

"What's your name, sweetheart?" I asked.

"I don't have to tell you my name."

A smart-ass. Great. What was I gonna do now? Play cop.

"Lady, this is a missing-persons case. You can give me what I need right here, or I'll drag your pretty ass down to the precinct and we can talk to my captain together."

Total bullshit. I couldn't haul her anywhere. This wasn't even close to a homicide and I didn't have paper. All I had was a raging hard-on. Somehow I didn't think a stiff dick was gonna get me what I wanted.

"Okay, okay. My name is Carla Amato and I don't know where Hank is. He was supposed to show up two weeks ago and never did. I keep coming in hoping he'll turn up. He's pulled this vanishing act before, so I'm not sweating it."

"I'd think you'd sweat your paycheck," I continued.

"I don't sweat that. I always get paid one way or another."

I wondered what the hell that meant, but I wasn't gonna find out. I kept staring at this goddess. I could practically see her rosebud nipples poking through the sheer blouse and that tight ass straining the fabric of her slacks. This lady dressed to make cocks stand up and salute. Low-cut silk top, pants so snug she could barely bend, just the right smoky eye shadow, sweet perfume, hand cocked on her hip like she was daring every guy who walked in to come over and grab a handful. This could be my kind of trouble.

"Ms. Amato, Mrs. Rossi said you might let me take a

peek at some of Mr. Rossi's client files to see if anything jumps out that could help me find him."

"She did, huh? Interesting. I really don't have the authority to hand over that stuff. Mr. Rossi is my boss. If he finds out I gave police access—even to a cop—he'd can me on the spot. This is a decent gig and I'm not looking to pound the pavement again."

"Well, Mr. Rossi can't fire you if he's not here, and if I don't find him you're gonna be out of a job anyway. So how about it?"

"Officer, I don't have the right to give you those files. They're confidential. Client privacy—ever hear of it?"

"Yeah, lady. I've heard of it. But this is a police investigation and client privacy, quite frankly, doesn't mean shit."

Not exactly professional, but what the fuck. The broad was driving me nuts and my brain wasn't working right. Actually, she looked a little turned on hearing a cop drop the F-bomb on duty.

"Officer, I just can't let you have Hank's files. I can't."

"Ms. Amato, I'm done arguing about the files. We'll deal with that later. You willing to answer a few questions?"

"Yes, I suppose I could do that."

Finally. Progress.

"Now that we got that straight—you said your boss has disappeared before. What's the story?"

"Well, Hank—Mr. Rossi—travels a lot. There are plenty of times he's not in the office. Usually he tells me when he's got a business trip, but sometimes he gets so buried he forgets to mention it. I figure he's just on one of his little getaways."

"You never see anything weird going on around here?"

"Something weird in an accounting office? Excuse me, officer, you gotta be kidding. The only thing that moves in here is adding machines and paper clips."

"No interesting clients?"

"Let's not go back to that, okay? I told you I can't talk about Mr. Rossi's files."

Worth a shot. What the fuck.

Carla started pacing the office and I was getting a major charge watching her hips roll. I could tell she was getting off on me watching her. Another exhibitionist. Just what I fucking needed.

"Ms. Amato, what do you know about Hank's personal life? You willing to talk about that?"

"I'm Mr. Rossi's secretary, not his marriage counselor. I know he's got a wife and a brother he's tight with. That's it."

This interview wasn't getting me anything but a bigger hard-on. Time to go for broke. "Ms. Amato, you busy today?"

"No, not really."

"Can I buy you lunch?"

"Well… okay."

I was getting somewhere. I just didn't know where yet.

Carla said, "There's a decent Chinese place around the corner. How's that sound?"

It sounded like shit, but I nodded. "Yeah. Great. Let's go."

Down the stairs and into the steaming August heat. I hoped the joint wasn't far. I was about to melt like a hooker on the Deuce after a long night.

It wasn't far, and the place didn't look half bad.

A little guy showed us to a booth and handed over a menu the size of the Daily News. I said, "Pick something for me. I'm not big on Chinese."

"This guy can cook anything. How about beef with ginger?"

I wanted to give her a little beef with pussy. "Yeah, that'll be fine."

We made small talk the whole lunch while I stared at her tits. Couldn't get a fucking word out of her about Hank or his problems.

Lunch came and by then I was playing footsie under the table. I rubbed her legs with the balls of my feet. I wanted to eat her cunt, fuck the beef with ginger. How about Harlan with Amato?

We survived lunch and I walked her back to the office. It wasn't getting any cooler and I had to yank my tie loose to keep from choking. By the time I climbed those stairs again I was panting like a dog. Was she gonna mistake it for lust? You bet your ass she did.

Carla perched on the edge of her desk, legs crossed. Those slacks were so tight I could see the outline of her pussy lips. No wonder she was horny—the fabric had been grinding her clit all day.

She raised one hand, crooked a finger at me. "You've been staring at me since you walked in. You think I'm pretty, don't you?"

I didn't choke this time. "I think you're fucking sexy."

"Would you like to fuck me, officer?"

I couldn't believe my ears, but I wasn't gonna argue. Instead of talking like an idiot, I ran my fingers across the front of her crotch. She arched back so I could reach better.

Her slacks were already damp. This broad wanted cock, and I wasn't about to say no.

"What do you want?"

"I want you to eat my pussy."

I reached up, undid her button. She lifted her ass and I slid the slacks down. Pants, shoes, everything hit the floor. Now I had a great American beauty sitting on a desk, legs spread, ready for my tongue.

I looked up. Black lace teddy under the slacks. Dark bush peeking around the crotch. Fuck.

I dropped to my knees and started kissing her mound. I could smell her perfume right through the lace. I ran my tongue over the fabric, down her slit. Two fingers massaged inside her thighs while I kissed up her belly.

One hand slid under her blouse, cupped a tit. Rock-hard. Nipples trying to punch through the lace. I unbuttoned the blouse. She lifted her arms one at a time so it fell away. Then she braced both hands behind her on the desk and shoved her cunt toward my face.

I kept kissing, massaging. Tongue probed her navel,

then lower. Back and forth over her lips through the lace. Heat pouring off her.

I didn't want her coming too quick, so I kissed up her body again. Lips pressed the teddy from navel to neck. Tongue snaked around her throat, licked behind her ears. She moaned.

I pushed my tongue in her ear. Goosebumps everywhere. Then back down.

Hands on her tits, pinching nipples. They got harder. She strained against the teddy. Wanted it off.

My mouth kept working. Tongue all over her belly, back to her pussy. Along the lace edges, down the inside of her thigh, around the back of her knee.

I lifted her ankle, ran my tongue from heel to thigh. Her teddy was soaked now. Pussy lips swollen, pushing against the lace.

I slid fingers under the crotch. Hot juice coated my hand. Her cunt was on fire.

Carla arched back. "Take it off. Touch my pussy with your tongue. Quit teasing me. I want your tongue on my cunt."

I pushed the pace. Shoved the teddy aside, massaged her lips. Fingers slid along the top of her slit. Lips swelled harder. Juice poured onto my hand.

"Play with me. Put your finger in my cunt. Fuck me with your fingers."

I plunged one in. She rode it hard. "I want you to fuck me. I want to feel you inside me. Touch me. You're making me so fucking hot. Quit teasing. I want to come. I want your cock."

I pulled my finger out, covered her cunt again. Disappointment flashed across her face. Too bad. I wanted to see how crazy I could drive her.

"You want me to fuck you? Want my tongue on your pussy and make you come?"

"Yes. Make me come. I want your tongue. Quit teasing and quit making me suffer. I want you to really touch me. Take the teddy off and let me come."

I wasn't done with the cop harassment. She got off on the dirty talk. I was gonna talk her into a screaming frenzy before I gave her the relief.

"What's wrong, baby? Getting horny? Like the way I touch you? Like my fingers fucking your pussy? Want me to make you come? Poor baby. You hot?"

"You son of a bitch. Quit teasing me. You talk like that and I get hotter and you won't do shit. You don't have any right to tease me. You're driving me crazy. I said I want you to fuck me—so fuck me and quit playing games."

I didn't want her pissed, but I knew I could push her a little more.

"Carla's getting hot. What's the matter, baby? Pissed at me? Tough. I want to watch you suffer. I want to see your cunt catch fire. I want you so horny you'll scream and beg. I like your pussy just like this—horny and begging."

"Harlan. I'll give you what you want. You can have the files. Just make me come. Don't tease me anymore.

   

You want Hank's fucking files, take them. Take anything. Just quit teasing me. I can't stand it."

I pulled away completely, walked across the room. "You want to see my hard cock, baby? Want to see what I'm gonna fuck your pussy with?"

I reached for my belt. No strip show, but I took my time. My dick was about to rip the zipper. The longer I waited, the hornier she'd get.

Carla reacted fast. "You're teasing me again, you cocksucker. Come over here and touch me with your tongue."

She was almost lying flat back on the desk, pussy in the air, hands under her ass. Juice glistened on her thighs.

Belt undone. Fly open. Pants dropped. Cock straining the shorts, pointing straight at her dripping cunt. "You want to see my cock, baby? Want me to fuck you? Want my tongue on your pussy?"

"Yes. Yes. Please. Let me see your big cock. I can tell it's beautiful. I want to see all of it."

I peeled the shorts off, kicked off shoes. Shirt next. Naked, hard, across the room.

"You like what you see? Like my cock? Want it in your hot pussy? You gotta beg for it. What are you gonna give me if I fuck you?"

"Anything you want. What do you want? Want me to suck you? Want me to finger your ass? Just quit teasing. My body's on fire. I can't wait. Fuck me."

"Now you know what I want, baby. You know exactly."

"I said you can have them. Take them. Take all of them. Just get over here and fuck me."

"Take all of what? What are you giving Jack for fucking your pussy?"

"The files. Take the fucking files. Do anything. Just quit teasing and fuck me. I want your tongue on my clit. My clit is begging. I'm so horny. I'm burning up. My pussy's on fire. I'm soaking. I want you. I want you to fuck me and make me come."

"Okay, baby. I'll make you come. Want to come? I'll let your hot cunt come on my mouth, then I'm gonna fuck you till you scream. Want my finger in your asshole. Want my tongue on your cunt. Ready, baby? Ready for me to fuck you?"

"Yeah, baby. Fuck me. Put your cock in my pussy. Rub my clit with your tongue. Make me come."

I crossed the room, buried my nose in her crotch, opened wide, shoved my tongue against her cunt. Perfume strong, love juice sweet on my tongue. I grabbed the teddy snaps with my teeth, yanked. Tongue plunged into her steaming hole.

Carla went wild. "Oh, you're so hot. So good. I love your tongue. Fuck me with your tongue. Push it inside."

My tongue plunged in and out. Each thrust, she shoved her cunt harder against my face. Pussy juice coated my chin, my cheeks. She was so hot I thought she'd explode.

"Eat me. Touch my clit. I want your tongue on my

clit. I want to come. Make me come. Oh Jesus. You're good. Make me come. Use your tongue."

I pulled my tongue down her crack, laid it flat, slid between fuck hole and asshole. She begged for her clit. I ignored it.

"Eat me. Put your tongue on my clit. Stop teasing, you motherfucker. You're making me crazy. Hotter and hotter. Stop it. I want your tongue on my clit. I'm gonna explode."

She grabbed my head, tried to force me up. I resisted. She kept pulling. I finally gave in.

I slid my tongue all the way down to her asshole, then up through her cunt to her clit. The button stood out, begging. I flicked it with just the tip. She pushed hard for more contact.

Juice ran down my face. Pussy got wetter. I worked her clit faster.

"That's it. So good. I like your tongue. Feels so good. Touch me harder. Faster. I want to come. Stop teasing. Let me come. Beat my clit. Faster. Faster. I want to come on your tongue."

I flicked harder, faster. Her clit throbbed, swelled huge. She pushed her pussy into my face.

"Fuck me. Oh Jesus. Oh God. Make me come. I want to come. That's it. Now you're doing it. Fuck me. My clit is gonna come for you."

No holding her back. Tongue beat her swollen clit. She shoved harder. Lips throbbed. Clit pulled back. Time.

"I'm gonna come. Harder. I want to come. My pussy's

throbbing. You're so good. Give me your tongue. Here it comes. Here it comes."

Spasms hit. Her hips lifted off the desk. Thighs shook. "I'm gonna come again. Never had it so good. I love your tongue. I can feel it coming again."

"Come, baby. Come for me. Come as much as you want. My tongue's yours."

Second orgasm hit harder. She screamed, "Oh God. Fuck it. Fuck it. I want your cock inside me."

I wasn't ready to fuck her yet. Too easy. She had another one in her. "I don't want to fuck you yet. You want my cock, you wait. I like my tongue in your pussy. Gonna keep licking your clit."

Angry moan. Sweetest cunt I'd tasted in years. I wanted more.

Tongue back on her crack, beating her clit. Button responded fast. She shoved her soaked cunt into my face again.

"Fuck me. Your tongue feels so good. Gonna make it come again. My cunt's gonna come all over your face. Want to taste my juices? I'm so horny. God, you're good. I'm gonna come."

I felt her clit ready, then pulled away. She snapped, "You bastard. Lick my clit. Why'd you stop? My pussy's begging. Don't make me suffer. All you do is tease."

I got off on her begging. I was in control. "What do you want? My tongue? Like it on your cunt? Like me making your pussy come? Too bad. I want to watch you suffer. I like hearing you beg."

I knew she couldn't take much more. I stood over the desk, reached for her pussy. Thumb and forefinger rolled her clit. It responded instantly.

Other hand plunged into her vagina. In and out, deep as I could. She rode my fingers. Soaking.

I let go of her clit, worked more fingers in. Two, then four. Coiled them inside her. Pushed.

She screamed, "Fuck me with your hands. Push your hand inside me. Harder. Fuck me harder. Shove it higher. Oh God, you feel good. Fuck me harder."

Juice ran down my arm. This broad was so horny it scared me.

I worked my second hand in. One finger at a time. She stretched, pleasure and pain. "Yes. That's it. Harder. Both hands inside me. Push. Fist-fuck my cunt. Make me come. Harder."

Couldn't push harder. Her box was stuffed. She screamed in pleasure, "You're so good. Fuck me. You asshole. Fuck me. My pussy's ready for your cock. I want your prick inside me. Fuck me. Fuck me."

I started pulling my hands out. Twisted fingers free. Her pussy relaxed. She was ready.

I stepped back, looked at her cunt. Lips so swollen they hid her hole. Juice everywhere.

I slid forward, pressed my raging cock against her. Lips grabbed me. I pushed past the muscles, felt the heat.

Slow strokes. She liked torture. I'd give her what she wanted. "Want my cock in your cunt? Want to feel my prick? Want me to fuck you?"

"Oh yes. Fuck me. I want your hot cock inside me. I want to feel you come in my pussy. Fuck me. Deeper. Fuck me."

Faster. Balls slapped her ass. She got hotter. "I want to fuck you. Like my prick in your cunt. Your cunt's on fire. Want to hear you scream. Like my hot cock? Want more?"

"Fuck. You're teasing again. Quit teasing and fuck me hard. Let me feel your prick all the way up. Give it to me hard. I want your burning cock."

Her talk was getting to me. I slammed deep, hit bottom, kept pushing. She screamed passion. "Yes. Oh God. Harder. Stretch my cunt. I want your prick all the way. Fuck me. Harder. Oh God."

I pulled back, then hammered fast. I wanted to come. "Your pussy's hot, baby. My cock wants to come in your pussy. Aching for you."

Cock ready to burst. Heat rubbed my shaft. Pulsations started. Jism flowed. "Yeah, baby. Gonna come. Want my hot load in your box? Want to feel me come? Like my hot rod?"

"Yeah. Come for me. I can feel it. Fuck me harder. Spray me. Come for me."

I collapsed on her chest. Muscles gone. Head on her belly, kissed her navel. Cock limp, but tongue still hard.

I slid up to her tits. Nipples swollen, waiting. Tongue circled one. Tissue hardened. I flicked. She rose again, horny.

Mouth over the nipple, rolled it between teeth. Bit

down. She responded, "Suck my tits. Bite them. Harder. You're making me horny again. My pussy's getting wet. Suck my tits. I want your mouth."

I bit harder, rolled. Other hand massaged the second tit. Nipple erect instantly.

"That's it. Touch my tits. Making me so horny. Suck them harder. Use your teeth. Pinch my nipple."

I glanced down. Her fingers snaked into her pussy, rubbing. Juice glistened.

"I want to play with my pussy while you suck my tits. Want to see me rub my cunt?"

Reminded me of another time. "Yeah, baby. Show me. Let me watch you rub your cunt. Want to see you make yourself come."

Mouth back on her tits, pulling. Tongue fast over nipples.

"I like rubbing my cunt for you. Gonna make myself come. Can I?"

"Yeah, baby. Make your horny cunt come. Make your pussy throb. Want to watch you rub your clit."

Her fingers circled her clit. Two flat, making circles. Button hardened.

Hand moved up and down, fingers plunging into her flaming pussy. I kept biting her tits while she got hotter. "I like to fuck myself. Gonna rub my clit and come. My clit's so hard. Want your mouth on my tits. Help me come."

I bit hard. She screamed with pleasure. Puddle of juice

under her ass. She bounced, threw herself up and down. "Gonna come. Gonna come."

Fingers plunged deep. She collapsed, eyes rolled back. Screaming nonsense. Cunt throbbed around her fingers. Powerful orgasm. When it finished she lay spent under me.

I stood, brushed hair from her face. Sweat on her forehead. She looked pleased. I hoped she'd keep me pleased.

I dressed while she stayed splayed on the desk. Loved the sight of her swollen, dripping pussy, but I was too wrecked to get it up again.

When she finally got up and dressed, I took the chair and watched. Beautiful sight—a satisfied woman in her underwear in an accountant's office. Who said accountants are boring?

Once she was dressed I went back to cop mode. The city wasn't paying me to fuck on their dime. Too bad.

"You promised me something."

"You can have anything you want."

"All I want is a look at the files. You said I could look."

I'd tamed the wildcat. She bought it. "Okay. I'll get them, but you better have them back in a day or two. I don't want Hank coming back and finding them gone. I can't lose this job."

I thought: if this broad puts out like this for every client and Hank, the only thing she's gonna get is a sore cunt.

She handed me a stack of maybe a hundred file

folders. No fucking clue what I was looking for, so I took the whole pile. My idea of a great night: thumbing through some asshole's tax returns for the last five years.

Oh well. Without Ramirez I had to start somewhere. This was as good a place as any.

I stuffed the files under both arms and headed for the door. This mess was gonna get messier when I started digging. Carla followed me out. I leaned over, planted a quick kiss on her forehead. "Thanks, baby. I'll get these motherfuckers back to you in the next few days."

Carla acknowledged my kiss and looked at the files like she was having second thoughts. I decided that I had better get the fuck out of there before her pussy dried out and she came to her senses.

I shoved the door open with my shoulder and hit the street.

# CHAPTER SIX

The battered Plymouth was waiting for me in the lot like a faithful old whore. I could spot that heap of shit from the other side of the Brooklyn Bridge on a foggy night. There was only one left in the whole fucking city and I owned it. Tourists used to wander up and ask me what the hell it was. I got so goddamn sick of explaining I slapped a hand-scrawled sign in the rear window: THIS IS A '49 PLYMOUTH FURY—KEEP YOUR FUCKING HANDS OFF. Now I don't waste breath on morons about my ride. Now I waste breath on missing persons.

What the fuck was my life coming to?

I tossed the stack of files onto the passenger seat and dropped my ass behind the wheel. I was one beat-to-hell son of a bitch. Every time I turned around lately I was staring at another set of tits or another shaved snatch being waved in my face. Was 1983 the goddamn Year of the Flasher? Looked that way. I wondered if I could wangle a transfer to Vice. Fat fucking chance with the budget cuts and three police commissioners in four years.

I stared at the pile of manila folders and wondered what the hell I was supposed to do with them. Somewhere in that mess there might be one tiny, stupid shred of something useful, but I didn't know what I was hunting for or where to start. Plan A was dump the whole stack on my desk at Midtown South and see if anything crawled out and bit me on the ankle. Plan B was haul the shit down to 1 Police Plaza and let Ramirez run it through the fancy new computer system in the basement.

I stomped the starter until the old girl coughed to life and pointed her nose back toward the precinct. The interview with Angela had been productive in its own wet, sticky way, but I didn't need to fuck my brains out for the second day running. Time to at least pretend I was doing some actual police work. Missing Persons police work? Yeah, right.

I trudged up the stairs to the squad room and there was motherfucking Captain Malloy waiting like a hemorrhoid that wouldn't quit. He didn't look happy.

"I wrote the goddamn report on my cruiser for you," he growled.

"Thank you, Captain."

"Thank me, my ass. You let my fucking car get trashed and now I gotta fill out the paperwork. What the hell do you think you are, Harlan?"

"Just a cop, sir."

"Fuck you. Sign this motherfucker and get your lazy ass on the Rossi thing before that Fred Rossi prick calls me again and I drive out to Bensonhurst myself and add his sorry ass to the Missing List."

I figured it was smart to look busy. The Captain was in full froth. Couldn't really blame him. The poor bastard loaned me his ride knowing exactly where I lived—Alphabet City, Avenue C, where cars disappear faster than hookers on 42nd after a bust. He was lucky the damn thing lasted till morning. Mine only survives because there are so few '49s left that chop shops don't even know what the parts are worth anymore.

I swaggered over to my desk, making damn sure the Captain didn't see how much he'd rattled me. Give the man a little rank and he starts thinking he owns the place. Big mistake.

Then I realized I'd left the fucking files in the car.

I shot a quick glance—Malloy was gone—and hauled ass back down to the lot. Files retrieved. Back at the desk I dumped the whole pile in one messy heap. I didn't know where to begin, but from what I'd seen so far there was something rotten about brother Hank, and those tax files were as good a place as any to start digging for the stink.

About fifty goddamn folders, and since I'd dropped the stack halfway up the stairs they were in total chaos. If there'd been any order once, there sure as shit wasn't now. I grabbed the first one. Hunter. Nothing but ten years of 10-40s. Guy barely made enough to eat and still paid an accountant. Maybe he couldn't count. Whatever. Useless.

The next ten were the same crap. Joe Schmo, too lazy or too dumb to fill out his own forms. I'd fucked my cock raw to get these bastards and there better be something in here worth the trouble.

I was reaching for number eleven when I caught Detective Morales drifting past my desk. The guy always smelled like he'd been marinating in garlic, but he was a solid cop. We hadn't spoken in over a year. He leaned in.

"I hear you're working the Rossi thing."

"Yeah," I said.

"Thought you might wanna know big brother ain't the saint he pretends to be. Back when I was in Vice—before they dumped me in this toilet—I pinched Fred Rossi for screwing minors."

"Really?"

"Really. Your guy. Looks like Joe Citizen, but he's bent as hell. I did everything short of kidnapping to get that little girl of his away from him. Couldn't prove shit. Authorities wouldn't buy it."

"Thanks. I'll look into it."

I appreciated the tip. So Fred was a kiddie-fucker. I had zero use for that kind of slime. This precinct could burn down around me and I wouldn't piss on it to save the place. Didn't know yet how it tied to Hank's vanishing act, but I was damn sure going to find out.

Tried to focus on the next file but my brain kept circling back to Freddy and Hank. Poor perverted Fred. Maybe Hank knew and was threatening to rat him out. Maybe Fred got too close to one of Hank's secrets. Maybe they were partners in something filthy and Hank wanted to walk. Somewhere in this shit-storm there had to be a thread. I'd pull till it unraveled.

File eleven: boring as a pimple on my dick. Some paint-store owner too dumb to do his own books. Same for thirteen through twenty. I was bored out of my skull but at least it looked like I was earning my paycheck. Maybe worth it just to keep Malloy off my nuts.

By twenty-five I needed a break. I decided to ring

Tina. We had a date tonight and I wasn't about to break it.

She picked up on the first ring. "Hi."

"Hi, hot cunt. What you doing?"

"Sitting here dripping, waiting for you. How's the case?"

"It's a motherfucker. This prick's brother likes them young, and I'm buried in tax returns. About to put me to sleep. Last thing I wanna do is stare at some asshole's 10-40 from 1968."

"Want me to wake you up?"

"Yeah, baby. Wake me the fuck up."

Tina started pouring the filth right into my ear. "I want you over here licking my pussy till I scream. I need that fat cock of yours. I went one whole night without your meat and I can't take another. Come fuck me stupid."

"I'll be there, you little slut, but duty's got me by the balls. Malloy's riding my ass because his cruiser got trashed in my driveway last night. If I don't get my shit together I'll be chaperoning senior proms next week. Four more hours and I'm yours."

"My cunt's soaking just thinking about it. Hurry."

"I'll be hard and ready, sexpot." I hung up and went back to the pile.

Things stayed dull until file thirty-five. That one had more than Salvation Army write-offs. Hank baby was doing books for the mob—or at least one of their made guys.

Vito Moretti. Big-time prick. The department had

been trying to nail the bastard for everything from racketeering to spitting on the sidewalk for twenty years. Witnesses vanished. D.A. dropped charges. You name it. Vito was a soldier for the big boys up in the Bronx and Jersey. Ran dope up the BQE, handled numbers in Brooklyn, whatever dirty job they threw him. Head so far up the family's ass he'd never see daylight till they dumped him at the gates of hell.

I wondered what the fuck Hank was doing cooking this guy's taxes. The returns looked clean on paper—come on, you don't declare heroin income. Still, Vito had heavy friends. Maybe Hank knew something he shouldn't. This one was definitely going to Ramirez.

The rest of the stack was routine garbage. Until I hit Hank's own return.

The dumb shit had filed his own taxes through his own office.

Who am I to complain.

I read them and holy shit, they were entertaining. Hank wasn't the saintly family man everyone wanted me to swallow. He owned Fred's ass lock, stock, and barrel—house in Bensonhurst, car, credit cards, the works. Hank was loaded. Fred was riding the gravy train. With big brother gone, no more handouts. Fred might actually have to work for a living. What a goddamn tragedy.

So what did I have? A mobbed-up accountant who bankrolled his freak brother, cheated on his wife, and vanished. Brother had an exhibitionist daughter. Accountant had a nympho secretary. One fucked-up family. Not exactly Leave It to Beaver, but technically the guy was still just missing. Still, the stink was getting stronger.

The rest of the files gave me nothing new. Same old shit.

I started thinking about Hank's side action. I still hadn't pinned down who his regular piece was, and guys always spill everything to the woman they're fucking. Find the chippy, I'd find the rest of the puzzle.

Another trip to Fred's place seemed like the move. Plus it got me the hell out of the squad room and away from Malloy's stink-eye.

I signed out and drove back to Bensonhurst.

Freddy opened the door like he'd been camped behind it. "You find Hank?"

I stuck out my hand. He ignored it. "No, but I found out a whole lot of other shit. Mind if I come in?" Didn't matter if he minded. I was coming in anyway.

He stepped aside. I took the same chair as yesterday, wondering if Bianca was warming up for another flash. I wasn't buying the innocent act today, but the fantasy was still sweet. I cut right to it.

"Mr. Rossi, you fucking lied to me. I don't like liars."

"What are you talking about, officer?"

"You got more than a brotherly interest in finding Hank. He's your goddamn meal ticket."

"How dare you—"

"I'll talk to you any fucking way I want."

"So he helps me out with a few bucks. What's the big deal?"

"No big deal—except there's a fat annuity to you and your daughter if anything happens to him."

"You saying I killed him?"

"No, sir. Just saying if he turns up dead, you're gonna be right at the top of the list. I don't know if he's worth more to you in a box than walking around, but I'll find out."

"So what?"

"So what the fuck else you holding back? I'll start. Your brother keeps books for some very interesting clients. At least one interesting client. Your brother did taxes for a major mob guy. Did you know that?"

"I don't know shit about his clients. I stay out of his business."

"Yeah, wouldn't wanna rock the boat when he's feeding your lazy ass."

"If you keep talking to me like that I'm calling your superiors."

I wasn't shaking. If Fred knew Malloy he wouldn't waste the threat. I leaned in harder.

"Come on. You had lunch with him once a week. You didn't talk business? What the fuck did you talk about—the goddamn weather?"

"Our private conversations are none of your business."

"Like hell," I spat.

"We talked about broads, okay?"

That wasn't what I wanted, but it reminded me why I

came. "Yeah, by the way—you said Hank wasn't exactly faithful. Who was he fucking? And don't even try saying you don't know."

"That's none of your fucking business."

"Yes it is. Tell me nice or I'll beat it out of you."

"All right. Last I heard it was that hot piece in his office. That broad'll fuck anything that holds still long enough. Hank said she was the hottest thing he ever had."

Sounded too easy, but I'd let it ride for now. Time for the real dirt. "Okay, Fred. I'll buy it till I check. Now the real shit. You're a con. You've got something to hide."

"What the hell—"

"Don't play stupid. You're the lowest scum breathing and if I hear any more bullshit I'll drag you outside and stomp your balls flat."

He flinched. "It was a frame."

"Frame my ass. You like little kids. You've been busted more than once. What's the deal? Hank paying you to stay away from playgrounds?"

"Hank isn't paying me shit."

"I'll bet. Did Hank know about your little hobby?"

"Hank knew it was a frame. Some bitch said I banged his daughter. She got her friends to lie. Made me look like the biggest pervert in the city. I didn't do a fucking thing."

"Sure. Two juries said different." I had checked after Morales clued me in. "You did ten hard years. Surprised you're still breathing. Guys like you don't last a week inside. Wonder if Hank and his mob pal had anything to do with that. I don't know what your game is, but I'm gonna burn it down."

I had nothing left to say to the grieving brother. I hate baby-rapers more than I hate the job itself. I stood up. "I'm done here. I'll be back. Don't try anything cute."

"Like that 'don't leave town' bullshit?"

"Yeah. Like that."

Cops actually say that crap. I felt like a clown even thinking it. Whatever. Nobody's perfect.

I slammed out of the house and felt like I needed to scrub my skin with lye.

Technically I still had an hour on the clock. I decided to swing by Hank's Midtown office again, confirm my suspicions.

Carla Amato was still there. She looked up when I walked in like she was already wet for round two. "Back so soon? Done with the files?"

"Not yet. Got another question."

"Yes?"

"I just talked to Fred. He says you and Hank were fucking. Any truth to that?"

She flushed, but didn't look away. "Yeah. We got it on a few times. Guess I couldn't keep it secret forever. But I really don't know where he goes when he's not here. We'd fuck on the desk sometimes, that's all."

For some reason I believed her. Something felt off, but I couldn't nail it down. I pressed anyway. "Your boss had some heavy clients. What do you know about them?"

"I told you—I never go into his files. I don't know the clients. They come in, I have them wait, he sees them. I don't ask questions. He pays me damn good. I keep my mouth shut, you know?"

Her silence and her hot pussy were worth a lot of cash, so I let it slide. If she was lying, Ramirez would catch it on the computer and I'd come back hard.

I thanked her, told her she could have the files back tomorrow, and headed home to Alphabet City.

# CHAPTER SEVEN

Home looked damn good after a day of interviews and total horse shit. My quick morning bang with Carla Amato was already wearing thin, and I was itching for Tina and that scorching, dripping pussy of hers.

By the time I pulled up to my crumbling Victorian in Alphabet City, the neighborhood scumbags had dumped another pile of garbage right in my front yard. Nothing new, but it still pissed me off every single time. You'd think these assholes would figure out I'm a cop and I could haul their sorry asses in. But they're too fucking stupid, and I hate the goddamn paperwork. So I just picked up the trash and lived with it.

I went inside, cracked open a cold beer, and tried to shove the whole Rossi case out of my head. The damn thing was spinning in circles and I wouldn't have any real answers until I talked to Ramirez in the morning. Figured two beers might do the trick to forget the fucking mess. But first I needed a shower before I headed over to Tina's place.

The shower felt fucking fantastic. I've got this giant old clawfoot tub in the place. I stand up and rinse off, then stretch out in that six-foot motherfucker and just soak. By the time I climbed out I was refreshed and my cock was already half-hard thinking about Tina. I hoped she was as ready as I was.

I dressed for the occasion — no shorts, just tight jeans that showed exactly what I was packing. I wanted her to know I was coming loaded and ready to fuck. I jumped in my beat-to-shit Plymouth and headed for her cheap walk-up in Hell's Kitchen.

Every time I pulled up to that cracker-box tenement of hers I wanted to scream. Tonight was no different. The building looked okay from the street until you got close and saw the cracked bricks and sagging fire escape. I worried about her. I was scared the whole fucking thing was going to cave in on her pretty head one night. I'd never been able to talk her into moving in with me, but I was ready to try again. Nobody should have to live like this. They should live with the real New Yorkers — pimps, junkies, and hookers working the streets.

I was a little early for our date, but I didn't give a shit. I had a key and no problem using it.

I walked down the narrow hallway and let myself in. I could hear the shower running. Figured she was getting ready for me. Best move was to join her. I stripped as I went, dropping clothes on the floor, and pushed open the bathroom door. Cheap plastic shower curtain, but it was pulled back enough to give me a perfect view of her gorgeous body. I could see the shadow of her big jutting tits through the curtain. Her hands were sliding up and down her front, and I watched her slip a soapy finger right into her cunt.

I walked over, yanked the curtain aside. Tina didn't

even flinch. She'd probably been standing there for the last hour waiting to "surprise" me. I decided to play along.

I stepped over the edge of the tub and into the hot spray. I slid my left foot across and stood right behind her. She acknowledged me immediately, voice husky: "I thought you'd never get here, Harlan."

"Oh baby, you know I can't go a whole day without this hot pussy."

I reached around and started massaging her heavy breasts. Her nipples stiffened instantly under my fingers. I pinched them between my thumbs and forefingers, rolling them hard. Tina shoved her round ass cheeks back against my cock, which was already swelling fast. "Oh, Harlan… you feel so fucking good."

I wasn't really into the whole shower fuck routine, but soap and water always made Tina extra horny. What the hell — sometimes you gotta give a broad what she wants.

I let go of her tits and slapped both hands hard across her ass. Tina jumped like she wanted to get away, but she was faking it. I spread my palms over her cheeks and started kneading them. She pushed back against me right away. "You like rubbing my ass? You know you do. You're getting me so hot, Harlan. My pussy's already dripping just from that."

"Yeah baby, I know. You love it when daddy plays with your ass. Want me to wash you?"

"Yeah baby. Wash me. Get me all clean so you can shove that horny tongue deep in my cunt."

I grabbed the bar of soap, worked up a thick lather

between my hands. Suds oozed between my fingers. When I went to set the soap down I "accidentally" dropped it on the tub floor.

Tina bent over to pick it up and I took full advantage. I slid my soapy hands between her ass cheeks. Her tight pink asshole winked up at me, begging to be fucked.

She set the soap on the edge and leaned forward, hands on the faucet. I kept rubbing my slick fingers up and down her crack. She started grinding back against me. I pressed a finger against her puckered hole and felt the strong muscle relax. Tina pushed harder. I slid my finger straight into her tight asshole. She moaned instantly, "Oh Harlan… you gonna fuck my asshole? I love it when you stick your finger up my ass. You gonna play with my butt?"

"Yeah Tina, I'm gonna finger-fuck your ass. Gonna push it as deep as I can. You want that?"

"Yeah baby… yeah! Fuck me. Oh that feels so good. I love your finger up my asshole. Play with my butt hole. I want to feel you inside my ass."

She was totally relaxed now and my finger slid easily in and out of her bung. Tina kept slamming her ass back against my hand, and every time she did I drove my finger deeper into her rectum.

I could see her knuckles turning white on the faucet. She was getting too hot too fast. Time to slow it down. Tina wasn't happy: "You cocksucker! Why'd you stop? You know I love your finger buried in my asshole."

"Easy baby. You know what happens when I really

   

work your ass. We're just getting started. Relax, honey. Hard Harlan's gonna take real good care of you."

I grabbed her hips and turned her around to face me. Warm water cascaded over my face and ran down her big tits. Her nipples were rock-hard, red buds standing out, begging for my mouth.

I leaned down and sucked one fat tit into my mouth, tongue swirling around the swollen nipple. I grazed it with my teeth and it got even harder. Tina groaned, "Suck my tits… your tongue feels so good. Lick my nipples. You're making me so fucking horny. I love your tongue on my boobs."

I kept lashing at her nipple while my hand slid down between her legs. Her cunt was soaked — water and pussy juice mixed together. Her clit was already stiff. I started rubbing it in slow circles while I sucked her tit. Her cunt lips swelled under my fingers. Tina was getting hotter by the second.

I pulled my mouth off her breast and took my hand away from her clit. She glared at me. "You asshole! Why do you keep teasing me? I love it when you play with my pussy and you're just fucking around. Harlan, you're such a prick."

"I'm a prick all right, baby. And this prick is about ready to fuck your cunt until you can't walk straight," I shot back.

I grabbed the soap again, worked up fresh lather, and started soaping her whole body. Bubbles slid over her tits, down her stomach, and straight into her dripping box.

I slipped a soapy finger deep into her cunt and started finger-fucking her hard. Her pussy walls clamped down on my fingers. I picked up speed, slamming them in and out. Tina was losing it: "Oh you asshole… fuck me! Fuck me with your fingers. Make me come. Shove your hand in my pussy and make it come. I want to feel you inside me. You're so good. I can't take much more. When are you gonna fuck me with that big prick? When are you gonna make my pussy explode?"

I pulled my fingers out again. I'd had enough of this stupid shower shit. I never saw the point in trying to fuck in the shower. I want to feel a real wet cunt, not a goddamn water park.

I turned her around so the spray could rinse the soap off, running my fingers up and down her spine while the water beat on her chest. When the suds were gone I reached over and shut the water off. I was already clean and starting to look like a prune.

Tina pouted. "You turned off the water."

"Yeah, I hate that shit."

"Well what do I get since I didn't finish my shower?"

"What do you want, hot pants?"

"I want you to fuck me. I want that hot meat buried deep inside me."

I wasn't about to say no. My cock was so hard I thought it might snap in half. "You got it, baby. I'll fuck you till you can't think straight. I'll make you come so hard your pussy melts."

I helped her out of the tub and grabbed a towel.

Nothing worse than trying to fuck a woman who feels like she just crawled out of a swimming pool.

It didn't take long to dry her off, and every swipe of the towel made her hotter. "I like that… I like when you treat me like your little girl. I like when you take control and show me you're gonna fuck me and make me come. I love feeling your hands on me."

When she was dry Tina leaned in and kissed me hard. I shoved my tongue into her mouth and felt hers fighting back. Her body was heating up again. I could already smell her pussy getting wetter. She was ready for the fucking of her life.

I grabbed her ass, lifted her clean off the floor, and carried her into the bedroom. That same soft pink light was on again. I hated the fucking thing, but it was better than the bitches who wanted to screw in total darkness. Tina was too horny to complain about anything now.

I tossed her onto the futon on her back and stepped back. I stood at the edge of the bed just looking at her. Pussy juice was already glistening on the insides of her thighs. She was soaked and ready, but I wasn't letting her off easy yet. "You want me to fuck you, baby?"

I felt a quick flash of Carla from earlier, but I shoved it out of my mind. This was my woman. The daytime bullshit didn't mean shit.

Tina licked her lips. "Yeah baby… I want you to fuck me. I want that hot prick slammed inside my pussy. I want to feel your thick cock stretching my cunt."

I moved to the foot of the bed and stared straight at

her dripping slit. She was getting more excited just from my eyes on her. Her cunt lips were swollen and dark, begging. I dropped my shoulders onto the futon and started sliding up between her legs. The sweet smell of her pussy made my angry cock throb even harder.

I stopped two inches from her cunt and just breathed on it. Her lips twitched. Tina was getting pissed. "Quit teasing me, you asshole! What the fuck are you doing? Put your tongue in my pussy. I want to feel that hot tongue on my clit. I need it now."

I moved closer and ran my tongue slowly along the edges of her cunt lips. They were burning hot. I pushed my tongue inside her hole, then pulled it back out, tasting her sweet juice.

Tina was shaking now. Her clit was sticking out, swollen and desperate. I flicked the tip of my tongue right across it. She jumped. "Oh that's good… your tongue is so fucking hot. Beat my clit with it. Make my pussy come."

I started licking left to right across her clit, faster and faster. Tina shoved her cunt harder against my face and arched her back off the futon. Her clit swelled even more. "Eat me! I love your tongue on my clit. Rub it harder. You're making my pussy so hot. I want to come. Eat my cunt until I come."

I sped up, lashing her clit relentlessly. I slid one hand under her ass and shoved a finger deep into her dripping pussy. Her walls were soaked and clutching at me. I added a second finger, fucking her harder while my tongue worked her clit.

Then I worked my other hand under her and slid my middle finger straight into her asshole. Tina slammed down on it. "Fuck my ass! I love your fingers in my asshole. Stretch me. Shove it all the way in."

I pressed my mouth tight against her cunt and flicked her clit even faster. Her pussy was gushing now, juice running down my chin and over my fingers. Her asshole and cunt were both squeezing me tight.

Tina started coming hard. Her cunt clamped down like a vice. "Fuck me! I love your tongue. I'm gonna come. Eat me. Fuck me with your fingers and make me come. I want it. I want it so bad."

I kept hammering her clit with my tongue and driving my fingers in and out of both holes. "You want to come, baby? You like my finger buried in your tight asshole? Gonna come all over my face?"

"Yes! Make me come. My pussy's burning up. Shove your finger deeper up my ass. Harder! Harder! I'm gonna come. I'm coming… oh God I'm coming!"

Her asshole tightened around my finger like a fist. Her cunt lips swelled huge and bright red. Juice flooded my face. She screamed at the top of her lungs, body shaking violently as the orgasm ripped through her. "I'm coming! My cunt is on fire! Oh God, Harlan… your tongue feels so fucking good. Fuck me harder. I'm coming so hard!"

I couldn't hold back anymore. My cock was throbbing, ready to explode. I yanked my finger out of her ass, slid up the futon, and pressed the fat head of my prick against her soaked cunt.

I teased her lips with it, sliding the head up and down her slippery slit. Tina was losing her mind. "You fucking bastard! Stop teasing and fuck me! Shove that cock in my cunt right now. I need it. Put it in. Fuck me!"

I couldn't take her begging anymore. I rammed my cock forward and buried it balls-deep in her burning pussy. Her hot juice coated every inch of my shaft as her cunt gripped me like a fist.

I started pounding her hard from the edge of the bed. "Yeah baby… I love my prick in your tight cunt. Your pussy's on fire. You love my fat cock stretching you, don't you?"

I climbed fully onto the futon, hands on her shoulders, pinning her down as I drove even deeper. My cock slammed in and out, faster and harder. "Your cunt feels so fucking good on my dick. So hot and wet. I can feel your pussy juice running all over my balls."

Tina was moaning nonstop. "Oh God yes! I love your hot cock. Fuck my pussy. Make me come again. I want to feel you shoot your load inside me. Give me that hot jism. Fill my cunt."

Her words were driving me crazy. I could feel my balls tightening. I tried to slow down but it was no use. The cum was rising fast. "I'm gonna come, baby. You want me to fill that pussy?"

"Yes! Come for me. Let me feel your cock explode inside me. Shoot it deep. I want every drop."

My cock started pulsing. I couldn't hold it. Thick ropes of hot cum blasted into her cunt, flooding her. I kept thrusting as I drained every drop, then collapsed on top of her, head on her shoulder. "Jesus Christ, Tina… you're so fucking good. You make a man lose his goddamn mind."

She wrapped her arms around me. I rolled to the side, still buried inside her. I don't even remember falling asleep.

# CHAPTER EIGHT

Morning. Fucking morning. I was so goddamn drained I could barely get my shit together. Tina had fucked me raw all night long and I was convinced my cock was officially retired for the rest of my miserable life.

Hell, I wasn't even sure the rest of me was still breathing. I lifted my head off Tina's sweaty shoulder and fought the urge to roll her over and drill her again. Captain Malloy was expecting my ugly ass up at Midtown South, and Ramirez probably had some answers waiting so I could dump this filthy Rossi mess once and for all, then haul ass back here and give my hot little number another deep pounding.

I dragged myself out of bed and stumbled into the shower. Standing under the weak spray, I kept replaying that filthy night and wondering what the hell it was about showers that turned a normal horny cop into a total fucking idiot. Couldn't find an answer, but my dick sure thought it knew — it was already twitching and thickening, ready for another slick round right there against the cracked tiles.

Too fucking bad. Wasn't gonna happen.

I'd been in there maybe ninety seconds when Tina slinked in behind me, pressing those big tits against my back. She wasn't interested in me doing my job, and neither was I. Too fucking bad. The job is the job is the job. I still valued what was left of my paycheck and I wasn't about to risk Captain Malloy's wrath. The guy might be a total chump, but he signed the checks, and unemployment would have my old man crawling up my ass — a way scarier prospect. I pushed her away, gave her the "I gotta go to work" speech, and got the hell out of that shower. Showers are dangerous. They make you stupid-horny. Maybe I should start taking baths.

Fuck it. Time to stop thinking with my balls and get my ass to the precinct.

I hopped out, dried off, and threw on yesterday's wrinkled clothes just in time to hear Tina whimper from the futon, "Take the day, baby. Fuck me some more."

I wanted to tell her I'd love to spend the next twelve hours balls-deep in her, but I knew it was bullshit. I walked back into the bedroom, gave her a quick kiss, and hit the street.

A job is a job is a job.

I wanted to be a mechanic. I wanted Fred and Hank Rossi to drop dead. I knew I wasn't gonna get that lucky, so the plan was simple: see Ramirez, find the hidden dirt, kiss Malloy's ass, and crawl back to where I belonged — between Tina's thighs.

My classic baby was waiting at the curb. She fired right up on the first try. Why the fuck couldn't the city buy decent cars? Stupid question. Look where the money was going — sending burnt-out assholes like me out to look for pricks who'd rather stay missing.

The ride uptown on the FDR was totally uneventful,

but the second I hit the top of the stairs at Midtown South I knew it was gonna be another shit day. Captain Malloy was tearing Detective Morales a new one. Poor fucker had only done his job, but Malloy was screaming that as a civil servant you don't just find a runaway kid, tell her it's in her best interest not to go home because her old man's a psycho, and then slip her a bus ticket to Miami. You just don't fucking do that.

Wrong. You bet your ass you do when you know the kid's going back to some animal who'll beat her bloody. You bet you do. Just because she's underage doesn't mean she isn't a human being. Malloy was dead wrong, but the stupid schlep had done one thing right in his life — he filled out the report on his trashed Plymouth and saved me the paperwork. I'd tell Morales to ignore the captain later. Right now I had to check in with Ramirez.

Malloy barked at me as I walked past, but I didn't even flinch. I'd learned to tune that prick out. If I dangled the Rossi thing in front of him he'd leave me the fuck alone.

I grunted something about having a hot lead on poor Hank and kept walking. The computer room down at 1 Police Plaza was starting to look good. Malloy never would.

Maria was looking fine as usual. Her tits were straining against that tight sweater like they were trying to escape. I don't know how the hell she wore those things in this heat, but if my cock's reaction was any indication, I would've glued the motherfuckers to my chest. I reached over and swatted her gorgeous ass, whispering in her ear,

"Whenever you're ready, baby. Let me take you to dinner and show you what real fucking is like."

She shot me down like always, but what the fuck. Someday. Someday. The broad couldn't hold out forever.

Ramirez was at his beloved terminal. I couldn't tell if he had a hard-on, but he was breathing like a guy about to blow his load, stroking the top of that computer like it was a wet cunt ready to come. I hated to interrupt whatever sick fantasy he was having, but I needed this Rossi shit off my back before Malloy shoved his dick up my ass and left me no place to sit.

"Hey, Ramirez, you got anything on that fucking Rossi thing?"

He didn't waste a second. "You bet your ass I do. This guy's a real motherfucker and you've got your work cut out for you. The whole family's fucked up, and from these printouts it looks like the best place to look for these assholes is the state pen."

I really didn't need this. I wanted it solved, not turned into some long-ass investigation. Why couldn't he just say he found poor Hank working as an evangelist in Pittsburgh? Or that Fred made the whole thing up and Hank was at an accountants' convention in Cleveland — preferably balls-deep in some secretary. No such luck.

"Okay, lay it on me. But take it easy — the last thing I need is a real job."

"Well, you got one this time, Jack. Fred — oh, Fred's a real piece of shit. Busted seven times in the last twenty years for humping little kids. Always skates. Jury gets tired.

Witnesses suddenly have to be at a swingers' convention out on the Island. The judge isn't interested. Super Bowl's on. I swear this prick could fuck your mother at high noon in Times Square with a video camera rolling and somebody would lose the tape before it hit the evidence room."

"Yeah, okay. Fred's a fuck, but I'm looking for his missing brother. I already know where Fred is. Hell, I even know what his daughter's cunt looks like."

"That's my whole point. You gotta know the family. Whatever happened to Hank is because of the sick shit that goes on in this clan."

"Okay, okay. Make your point." I wasn't in any hurry. I liked it down here, Maria was standing in the doorway giving me a nice view of her tits, and if he solved the case too fast I'd just get another one. Might as well stretch this one out.

"The daughter's a real piece of work too, but sounds like you've already had a good taste of Bianca's charms. That little slut's been in and out of institutions most of her life for exhibitionism. First five times in juvenile, then the state in its infinite wisdom sent her to the nut house. Did a lot of good — half the staff caught the clap from her. The chief administrator ended up hanging in his office from a pair of black pantyhose, for Christ's sake. Couldn't prove she did it, but her ass got released in a real hurry after that."

"Okay, so brother and niece are bent. What about fucking Hank?"

"Poor Hank. Looks like a solid guy on paper. Typical cheating-husband accountant. Boring as hell. Never even had a parking ticket, but he's got some interesting friends and habits. Hank's a motherfucker, but he's a lot smarter than Fred — he just doesn't get caught."

I could feel my ass heading for the wringer, but I couldn't see exactly how yet. This was starting to look like I might actually have to work. "Yeah, well I don't see any hard evidence against Hank. I know he owns his brother, but that don't mean shit. Maybe he got tired of carrying the prick and split."

"Harlan, that's a nice thought, but I've got enough printouts here to prove you've got your head up your ass if you keep believing that."

"Okay, okay. Hit me. I want to finish this motherfucker and get on with my life."

I glanced over at Maria again and wondered what it would take to get her into my bed. Had no clue, but it was a hell of a lot nicer fantasy than wondering what happened to poor Hank.

Ramirez was practically creaming his jeans to tell me what his magic box had dug up. "Hank's a middleman. Can't prove every detail, but there's enough here I'd bet my terminal he's in so deep he'll never climb out. One, he was there every single time Fred got busted, but nobody could ever hang anything on him. Two, he does the books for the mob."

"I already know that, and I figure it might explain where his ass is. So get to the point."

"I'm getting there. If you'd cool your jets. The mob guys he keeps books for are into porn — the ugly kind. They fuck kids, take pictures, and sell them to sickos like Fred. There's serious money in that shit. Serious money. And even more in keeping your mouth shut."

I almost told him I wasn't stupid — I'd worked Vice long enough to know the score. The pricks who made that filth would rather kill you than let you watch one of their movies twice. You might talk. So I kept my mouth shut and let him run.

"This Vito Moretti fuck is one of the worst. Hank's been doing his books for years, and no accountant is worth the kind of cash the bank records say he's getting paid. Add in that chippy secretary of his — the one with the record as long as your cock. Little bitch was a hooker for years. Fuck anything that moved. But when Vito Moretti's your pimp, you don't cross him or you end up the star of some snuff flick."

Things were looking worse by the second. Exhibitionist kids, pervert parents, hookers, dirty mob money. I was supposed to be chasing fifteen-year-old runaways who didn't want to get their asses beat anymore. If the city thought this was entertainment, they were wrong. I was about to get my horny ass buried in shit I didn't want and probably get killed over a lousy slice from Ray's. Why didn't these fucks just stay in whatever hole they crawled out of?

It's not mine to question why. I'm a fucking civil servant. They throw it, I catch it.

Too fucking bad.

"Okay. Good work, Ramirez. You've dug up a whole pile of ugly bullshit, but how the fuck am I supposed to put it together? Yeah, yeah, I know — you're just the computer guy. This part's on me."

Ramirez shrugged and went back to stroking his terminal. "You send me to do a job, I do the motherfucker. Now you do yours and everybody's happy."

Maria had walked back to her desk, but she looked up as I came out. "Ugly mess, isn't it, Harlan?"

"No shit. I don't know why the system doesn't just lock these freaks up and throw away the key."

"Me either. But I bet you don't find Hank alive. From what I overheard, I think he watched one too many of those movies and his friends decided it's time for him to spend the rest of his life under a football field in Jersey."

I tended to agree. But fuck — I wasn't Homicide. Looked like I was about to be. "I'm gonna have to think on this one, but you're probably right. Something really shitty's going on and my poor ass is stuck right in the middle."

Maria gave me her sexiest smile. "Tell you what, Harlan. You find Hank alive and I'll take you up on that dinner date."

I wasn't turning that down, even though I knew she'd kill Hank herself before she went out with me. Still, she was hot enough that I'd take the challenge. Stranger things have happened in this city. I figured if I could find Jimmy Hoffa, I could find Hank Rossi.

"Thanks, babe. I know this new Italian joint on Mulberry that'll make your toes curl." She looked at me like I was crazy. I just grinned. She had no idea I'd resurrect the poor bastard from the dead if it meant getting a shot at her hot pussy.

I took one last look at my motivation and climbed the stairs out of 1 Police Plaza. Looked like I had to go back upstairs and face Malloy for a while, but once he saw what I had, he'd stay the fuck off my ass until I dropped Hank's dead body on his desk.

# CHAPTER NINE

The squad room at Midtown South was a total fucking shambles by the time I dragged my ass back in. Captain Malloy was in full scream mode, veins popping, and the regular officers were scattering like roaches when the lights flip on.

I was the next poor son-of-a-bitch through the door.

"And you, Harlan! Where the fuck has your lazy ass been? This Rossi bastard is driving me up the wall and I'm sick and goddamn tired of hearing about his missing brother!"

"Captain, cool your jets. I've been down at 1 Police Plaza with Ramirez and it looks like I'm gonna wrap this motherfucker up quick. Fred and Hank Rossi ain't exactly saints. They're into kiddie shit. The secretary used to be a hooker and dear old Hank gets all his fat bucks from the mob. Looks to me like his usefulness has expired."

"Yeah, yeah. I don't wanna hear about it. Get your ass out there and do something, would ya?"

I didn't need another round with Malloy. He was fresh out of unmarked cars and I was fresh out of smart-ass comebacks. Time to end this shit.

Down the stairs, into the parking lot. My beat-to-hell Plymouth sat waiting. I wondered how the captain could be so pissed about losing one of his—mine was a rolling piece of garbage compared to anything else on the lot.

Still, it kept Hank, Freddy, and Bianca out of my head for a minute.

I climbed in, fired up the engine, and just sat there mentally jerking off. I still couldn't figure why Hank was bankrolling Freddy. Unless Freddy was taking the heat for him. And what the fuck was with that exhibitionist kid? Did Vito Moretti plant the secretary there, or did Hank request fresh pussy from the old stable? This whole thing was a confusing mess, but I was gonna get to the bottom of it.

Best place to start was right back with Freddy, baby. If the fucker had something to hide, why the hell was he riding the cops' asses every five minutes? Not too bright.

As usual the prick was home, ready to jump my shit because I hadn't found his brother yet.

"Harlan, do you give a fuck at all? If you don't care about people, why the fuck did you become a cop? You should've been a goddamn mortician!"

I wanted to plant my fist in his face. Too bad it was against the rules. Last thing I needed was a suspension for smacking a prick who deserved it.

I laid into him hard. "Listen, Rossi. This whole thing stinks worse than a Times Square dumpster in July. You're gonna get straight with me or I'm hauling your ass straight to the can and you can tell the whole fucking precinct what the hell is going on."

Freddy wasn't buying it. He'd been grilled by better than me, but I knew the weak link was Bianca. I could jack off with Freddy a little longer and all I'd get was righteous indignation, so I switched targets.

"Okay, prick. You think you're one smart son-of-a-bitch, but I'm gonna get your ass. You keep jerking me around and not only will I not find your precious brother, I'll make sure you end up on a missing-persons list that goes straight into the trash can."

He still wasn't buying, but as I turned to leave I caught my real target flashing ass at me from the hallway. Let her give me a good look at that young pussy and she'd spill enough that I wouldn't be running all over this rotten city shooting blanks.

I slammed the door and hit the sidewalk. Bianca wasn't far behind.

"Are you mad at Daddy? What'd he do to you?"

"He hasn't done shit, and that's the problem. He's so worried about Uncle Hank, but every time I ask him a question he lies through his teeth. I don't suppose you could help?"

Bianca gave me that little exhibitionist smile and said, "I really don't know anything about it. Uncle Hank just didn't show up for lunch one day. They eat together all the time. I know Daddy's more upset than Aunt Angela, but I can't tell you where he is."

"You can't tell me that, but I'll bet there's other stuff you can show me."

She took the hint immediately and started stroking herself right there on the sidewalk. I figured if she got lost enough in her little game I'd find something out.

"That's pretty, baby. Now just tell me what you can."

"I told you, he didn't come to lunch. They go to this special place downtown and he missed it."

Finally, something new. "What special place?"

"Oh, just some dive downtown they always hit. I really don't know the name."

She was getting hotter with her game and I gotta admit it was getting to me. My cock was thickening in my pants at the little show. I needed to know where the fuck they went for lunch. Wherever it was, I knew it was a shithole and the key to this whole stupid mess.

"Try and remember, honey. Where downtown? What's the name? Anything."

Her breathing was getting heavier, but she kept feeding me scraps to hold my attention. I was right.

"Down on Third Avenue. I know it's on Third, but I really don't know the name. Are you gonna watch me come?"

I wanted to say yes, but this was getting too sick even for me. Whatever weird disease was running through this family, I wasn't signing up to be part of it.

"No, baby. I'd love to look at your pretty little pussy, but I can't."

She looked crushed. I patted her now-soggy cunt, turned, and walked away.

A joint on Third Avenue. What a fucking neighborhood. Made my crumbling Victorian in Alphabet City look like a chunk of Park Avenue. Gay joints, bi joints, leather joints, S&M joints—every perversion in the book was on Third Avenue. I didn't have to be a genius to figure out what cookies Hank and Fred were eating down there. And there was only one place that even pretended to serve food: Slick's on 8th and 42nd, right in the heart of Times Square sleaze. My chances of walking in alone were about the same as getting Maria to fuck me on the hood of my Plymouth.

I wasn't doing this one solo. I needed a pro.

Carla Amato was sitting at her desk when I barged into dear old Hank's fifth-floor Midtown accounting office—the elevator still broken, of course. First words out of her mouth: "Where are the files?"

I wasn't interested in files. If my hunch was right she could have the motherfuckers back about the time she got out of Rikers. "I'm not interested in your fucking files, sweetheart. You lied to me and I don't like liars. Lying ex-hookers really piss me off."

She went white. "I ain't no hooker no more and you can't come in here acting like that. What's your fucking problem? You barge in like I took my boss out and killed him myself. Fuck, he signs the checks, baby. He's the best trick I ever had and I'm not fucking up the gravy train. Got it?"

I got it, but I didn't give a shit. "Listen, honey. You can turn all the tricks with grown-ups you want. Best pussy I ever had came from hookers. But this kiddie shit ain't gonna fly. Got it?"

"What kiddie shit? Have you lost your fucking mind? I got no idea what you're talking about."

"Listen, Carla, baby. You remember your old pimp Vito Moretti? He's got a sideline and his actresses and actors end up dead."

"Yeah, Vito was a weird motherfucker, I'll give you that, but why you riding my ass?"

"Give me a break. Hank does the fucker's taxes, you used to be in his stable, and now Hank's missing. Does that add up to you?"

"If you think I got anything to do with it, you're nuts. I quit that life years ago. Got this job straight—friend told me about it, I applied, and I don't know shit about any kiddie stuff."

I wasn't sure whether to believe her, but at this point I didn't have much choice. She was coming with me to check out that sleazy joint and I wasn't taking no for an answer.

"Listen, you're going with me and you're putting on your best hooker smile. I'm your favorite John and you're gonna show me a real good time. Give me one shred of shit and I'll bust your ass for anything I can think of and you can spend some quality time in the Tombs. Sound fun?"

"What do you need me for? You're a cop. Go wherever the fuck you want."

"Third Avenue, baby. You and me are going down on Third and find out what Fred and Hank were into. Get it right the first time. If you blow this I'll ride your ass till I find something to send you upstate. Got me?"

I had her attention. "Alright. Christ. You'd think somebody just shot the fucking Police Commissioner."

I leaned over the desk, grabbed her shoulder, and shoved her toward the bathroom. "Get your ass in there and dress the part. I'll be waiting." She tried to close the door. "Leave the fucking door open."

Ten minutes later we were rolling into Scummerville. Every lowlife in the city passed through Third Avenue sooner or later. The cops mostly left it alone—better to keep all the maggots in one garbage can than spread across the five boroughs. I thought it was sad how right at home Carla looked in that neighborhood.

Slick's had been on every vice squad hit list for years. Nude dancing, back-room action, and the owner had a known taste for babies but always skated the charges. We pulled up in front of the joint to see the barker hawking a nude hat-check girl who'd check more than your hat.

I pulled Carla out of the car and steered her to the door. She looked sleazy enough that the barker didn't sniff my cop vibe. One down, two to go.

Inside, the place would make a buzzard puke. The floor was sticky with God-knows-what. Cheap red lights flashed over the nude dancers on stage, bread crumbs from stale sandwiches everywhere. The bar was lined with ten sick fucks staring into the cunt of the girl on stage while the bartender couldn't decide whether to pour drinks or just jerk off with his eyes.

I walked Carla up to the bar and asked loud enough for the bartender to hear, "What'll you have, honey?"

I ordered for both of us and prayed the alcohol would kill whatever was floating in the glasses.

The broad on stage was a mess—more time scratching her heroin sores than dancing. She kept spreading her pussy lips and rubbing her clit like she was trying to start a fire. Some asshole in front reached up and fingered her while the rest of the crowd hooted like animals. I'd seen better-looking cattle on the BQE.

I couldn't watch much longer or I'd lose my watered-down swill. Lucky for me, Carla knew her role. She leaned in, rubbed my cock through my pants, and whispered loud enough for the bartender, "Hey, baby. Let's go do a thing in the bathroom. Mama's horny for that hot cock and doesn't wanna wait."

I reached around and shoved my hand up the crack of her ass, rubbing hard. "Yeah, baby. Get Daddy off. I'm so fucking horny. Is my little girl gonna take care of me?"

The bartender heard every word. We had him.

We got up and headed for the restrooms. We'd barely made the hallway when the bartender caught up. "Hey, buddy. Want something a little more exciting? I couldn't help hearing you and your lady. She's fine, but I got something that'll make it a lot hotter for both of you."

"Hey man, what the fuck? I paid for this lady—she's the best pussy around. What makes you think you got anything better?"

"Trust me, buddy. Bring your lady and you'll have the hottest time of your life."

I looked at Carla. "How much?"

"Hundred bucks."

"That's a lot of scratch for a come show."

"Best one you'll ever have," the bartender assured mel

"Yeah, sure. Okay, but it better be worth the C-note."

I paid the motherfucker and we got shuffled into the back room.

If the front of Slick's was sleazy, the back was worse. A cheap 16mm projector on a wobbly table, a wrinkled white sheet on the wall, metal folding chairs. I felt my stomach turn.

The creep said fifteen minutes and left. Carla and I sat while all kinds of sleazy balls and creeps filed in. I had a pretty good idea what was coming and I wasn't looking forward to it.

When the room was full the creep locked the door, killed the lights, and started the projector. Standard porno shit at first—blowjobs, pussy-eating, fucking. About twenty minutes in it turned nasty.

Some big black guy was pounding a white girl in the ass and she clearly wasn't into it. He didn't like that. He slammed her head into the wall and kept going. The flick got violent fast. The ass-rape went on for another ten minutes with the girl screaming while he slapped her face and yanked her hair.

Then the door on screen opened.

I almost pissed myself.

It was Bianca.

I'd seen enough. I grabbed Carla and bolted for the exit. The creep yelled, "Hey man, it's just getting good!"

"No thanks, buddy."

The little cunt had lied to me. When I got my hands on her she was gonna wish she was never born, and when I found the director of that little epic he was gonna be dead.

I yanked Carla into the car. She screamed, "Hey, what the fuck? You drag me to that dump, stick me in front of some sick movie, then toss me out like your ass is on fire. What the hell's going on?"

Either she was the best actress alive or she really didn't know. "Bianca Rossi. That was Fred's daughter in that motherfucker. Your boss and his brother are in the life. They're making snuff flicks—probably kiddie ones too—and any other scumbag entertainment that turns a buck. Got it now?"

She got it. I could tell she wasn't lying—she looked ready to puke all over my Plymouth. The bitch really had gone straight. "You coming with me or you want me to drop you?"

"Drop me. I've had enough of this shit."

I slowed to about three miles an hour and pushed her out in front of Hank's office, then headed straight back to the Rossi house in Bensonhurst.

Freddy was there as usual, but he wasn't getting away with any more crap. I kicked the fucking door in, grabbed the bastard by the hair, and slammed him into the wall. "Okay, motherfucker. Game over. Start talking or I'm blowing your perverted balls off."

Freddy wasn't so tough after all. I planted my size-twelve shoe against his nuts. He got the message fast. "Okay, okay! What the fuck—I report the cocksucker missing and suddenly I'm the criminal?"

"You are a criminal, prick, and one sick motherfucker. Putting your own daughter in porno flicks ain't gonna win you Parent of the Year."

"Fuck, man, I didn't make her do that shit. I got nothing to do with it. What the fuck are you talking about?"

"You know exactly what I'm talking about. Now spill or I'm crushing your balls like grapes."

"There ain't nothing going on."

I pressed harder. He got smarter quick. "Yeah, yeah—get your foot off my balls! So she made a movie or two. Nobody forced her. She's always been like that. What's illegal about making a movie?"

"Plenty when you're twelve fucking years old, asshole."

I kept my shoe on his sack while I grilled him. "Okay. Where's Hank? And don't tell me you don't know."

"I got no fucking idea. He's just gone. I guess they did something to him. I don't know."

"Who did something to him?"

"Vito Moretti. Vito owned his ass. The cocksucker tried to pull me in and I wouldn't play. He ruined my electrician business, probably killed my wife, and went after Hank. I didn't do nothing."

I knew the bastard was guilty as hell, but I didn't have enough for a clean case yet. I kept pressing. "What the fuck is really going on?"

"I don't know, I don't know!"

I stomped his balls again.

"Let me up! Let me up and I'll tell you anything!"

I yanked him up by the collar and pinned him to the wall. "Start talking and it better be good."

It was mostly bullshit, but enough. "Hank liked the kids, man. I covered for him for years. What the fuck was I supposed to do? He was my brother. Sure it's sick, but I took the rap once in a while. So what? Vito gave Hank his kid fix in exchange for tax work. Those two been at it fifteen years. I don't know exactly what they do."

"Now fill in the blanks, asshole. You like it too. You hang in the same sleazy joint. Why's Hank got all the money? What's he got on you?"

"Nothing. He ain't got shit on me."

The man was a lying sack of shit, but I had enough to hold him. I cuffed the prick to a heavy chair and called for a radio car. "This is Harlan. I need a black-and-white at the Rossi house in Bensonhurst for a prisoner transport."

They said it wouldn't be long. Translation: at least an hour.

Forty-seven minutes later they hauled Freddy away. I headed straight for Angela's tract house in Forest Hills. She knew more than she was letting on too. This whole fucking family was rotten and their little perversion party was about to end.

Angela answered the door quick. I asked to come in and she led me to the living room, all polite. "How can I help you, officer?"

It took everything not to smack the bitch. "Your brother-in-law's in jail on suspicion of murder and manufacturing obscene material. Seems he didn't mind putting your niece in a flick or two. What do you say about that?"

Something was off. I couldn't place it at first.

Then it hit me like a two-by-four.

No woman alive had an Adam's apple like that.

I grabbed "her." The face felt like sandpaper under the makeup. I reached down and squeezed a very real set of balls. "Okay, 'lady.' You're coming with me."

"What the fuck are you talking about? I haven't done anything!"

"Right, Hank. You and Freddy thought we were all stupid. Where's your wife, you fuck? What'd you do with her?"

"I don't know what you're talking about! Get your hands off me!"

That slightly husky voice I remembered turned into pure linebacker. This was the weirdest shit I'd seen in eighteen years on the job—a transvestite porno king. What the fuck was next?

I squeezed his balls harder. He screamed and turned green, ready to puke.

I had him.

Hank—dead? My ass. Good old rich, faggot, ugly Hank. He must've really loved baby brother Freddy. Figured poor Freddy wouldn't be poor anymore. The prick was gonna collect his own insurance, beat the mob, and run off with Freddy to sleazeball paradise.

They almost pulled it off. Too bad the poor bastard didn't own a decent razor.

I drop-kicked his perverted ass into his own living-room furniture and cuffed him to a chair. Then I called it in again. "This is Harlan. Our missing person ain't missing anymore. Send black-and-whites to the Rossi house in Queens—less than an hour this time."

Gonzales bitched about overtime but said they'd roll.

While I waited I decided to violate every right the prick had and toss the house.

The bedroom closet was a pervert's wet dream: double-headed dildos, pictures of people in every stage of dismemberment, photos of little kids with sick fucks like Hank and Freddy, video tapes, 8mm reels, stroke magazines. The guy had the world's largest pornography collection. Every perversion covered. He must've been wholesaling to the whole East Coast.

By the time I finished the house I still had the garage left. I'd already found enough to put Hank away for life, but since I was already shitting on the Constitution I figured I might as well finish the job.

Two cars, a ten-speed, and a couple of freezers.

I should've been so lucky.

The garage was packed with freezers. Either Hank was a serious meat eater or there was something on ice I wasn't supposed to see.

I opened the biggest one and my stomach flipped.

Angela. Wrapped and packaged like a fucking side of beef. Marinated in barbecue sauce. Labeled for dinner.

I leaned over and puked on the garage floor.

I heard the black-and-whites pull up.

Freedom. No more. Being a cop should be punishment for criminals. Nobody should have to do this shit. Nobody should work overtime either—overtime means finding a guy's wife in the freezer.

Two young patrolmen came to the garage door. I showed them the package. They turned white as sheets. Revenge is sweet. I told them to handle the reports and headed back to the precinct.

Captain Malloy was still pissed when I walked in, but not for the usual reason. "I hear you found Rossi?"

"Yeah. Dirty prick killed his wife and figured we were too stupid to look."

"I suppose you think your job's over now?"

"You bet. You sent me to find the motherfucker. I found him. It's after five and I got a date."

"You can take your date and shove it. You got more work. They booked Fred Rossi and his ass is singing like a canary. You brought him in, you interview him and get the full statement."

I was beyond pissed. The cocksucker worked me to death, got results, and now expected paperwork. I risked it all. "Fuck you, Malloy. My day is over and Freddy can stay on ice till morning."

Two-hundred-seventy-five pounds of blubber turned bright red. "Harlan, you get your ass to the Justice

Center and interview that man or I'll write you up for insubordination and make sure you never get off this fucking detail."

He had me. My date with Maria would have to wait. Images of my old man and Wyatt Earp ripping my face off sent me downtown.

By the time I got there, Freddy was ready to spill everything to save his own ass.

I sat down in the interview room. "Okay, prick. You're fucking up my date and this better be worth it. What's so goddamn important it can't wait till morning?"

"I want you to know what happened so you don't blame me."

The stupid fuck still hadn't figured out he and his brother were gonna take the fall for half the open sex-crime files in the city, and that me blaming him for ruining my pussy appointment was a far worse crime in my book.

"So get to the point."

"Hank made me. It was his thing. The money. All he cared about was the money. He'd do anything for a buck. I was just a dumb electrician, then he took me to that place."

"What place?"

"Slick's."

"What about Slick's?"

"The broads and the cards. I loved it. Couldn't stop. He kept getting me these hot chicks and I couldn't stop.

They had the hottest pussies I'd ever seen. What the fuck was I supposed to do? He had me."

It was hard to feel sorry for the louse. "Keep going."

"The money. I owed so much. Vito loaned me for pussy and cards, anything I wanted. I got in too deep. He wanted to collect and Hank wouldn't help. Can't you see they made me?"

I couldn't see shit except Maria's gorgeous tits and the chance at a world-class piece of ass. "Finish it, asshole."

Freddy turned white. "They made me. Vito said I could pay him back if I found him a girl for a movie. Young stuff. You know what happened. She was always like that. She was perfect."

I felt like puking but stayed quiet.

"I did what they wanted. It was never enough. I was always in trouble. No matter what I did, Vito had something else. He killed my wife. I know it. But the worst was the last movie. When that happened they had me forever."

"What the fuck do you mean forever?"

"They were gonna make a new kind of movie. They wanted a girl. I got one, but that wasn't enough. I owed a hundred grand and they were gonna cut my prick off and stuff it down my throat if I didn't deliver. They made me kill her. I didn't have a choice. They were gonna kill me."

I glared at the piece of shit. "You finished?"

He nodded. I called him scum and walked out.

Walking back to the precinct I had trouble not getting sick. What the fuck had the world come to? I didn't know what pissed me off more—working overtime when Maria owed me a fuck, or knowing Freddy would probably cut a deal with the Feds for what he knew about Vito and Hank and maybe even walk.

Up the stairs to Malloy's glaring face. I wanted to punch the fat fuck in the mouth. He loved overtime like it was pussy.

I sat at my desk. Malloy barked, "Did you get it?"

"I talked to the fucker, yeah. What an asshole. That shit isn't supposed to happen on this detail."

"So what'd he say?"

I wasn't giving him the whole thing. "You better get hold of the Feds. Looks like Fred's got enough on the mob they might want in. Other than that, read my notes. It's almost ten p.m. and I got a bet to collect on."

"I don't know what kind of bet you got, Harlan, but you're a cop first. Answer my questions or I'll have you looking for out-of-state license plates for the rest of your tour. Sound exciting?"

It sounded like shit. I passed anyway.

**THE END**